# JUST LIKE GREY 16

CALLUM REILLY

JESSIE COOKE

REDLINE PUBLISHING

# CONTENTS

*A Word from Jessie*   v

| | |
|---|---|
| Chapter 1 | 1 |
| Chapter 2 | 9 |
| Chapter 3 | 17 |
| Chapter 4 | 25 |
| Chapter 5 | 33 |
| Chapter 6 | 42 |
| Chapter 7 | 50 |
| Chapter 8 | 57 |
| Chapter 9 | 64 |
| Chapter 10 | 71 |
| Chapter 11 | 78 |
| Chapter 12 | 87 |
| Chapter 13 | 96 |
| Chapter 14 | 104 |
| Chapter 15 | 113 |
| Chapter 16 | 122 |
| Chapter 17 | 130 |
| Chapter 18 | 137 |
| Chapter 19 | 144 |
| Chapter 20 | 151 |
| Chapter 21 | 159 |
| Chapter 22 | 166 |
| Chapter 23 | 174 |
| Chapter 24 | 182 |
| Chapter 25 | 188 |

*More Books by Jessie Cooke*   199

# A WORD FROM JESSIE

**Just like Grey is an Amazon Best Selling Series.**

All books in the series are written for open-minded adults who are not easily offended, so you will encounter anything from cheating, explicit sex, unprotected sex, drug use, adult language, and many more topics that could upset the wrong reader.

These are not vanilla stories.

That said...I hope you enjoy it.

Happy Reading,

Jess

# 1

Callum could have taken the nine-minute taxi ride from the Chi-town Precinct to the northern border of New York's Upper East Side. But he chose the subway, which would take thirty. Not that he didn't have fifty bucks, but it was a waste of money. If there was anything useful his parents drummed into him, it was the value of a dollar. Callum learned when he fled the manicured lawn of Winnetka, Illinois, that there was no one cheaper than a millionaire, and this had shocked him. His buddies and brothers-in-arms, who had nothing but their field packs and maybe a football, were far more generous than his parents ever could be. For this, he would always love his old unit. But he had to push the memories of those guys to the back of his brain. Remembering the dead never cast the day in a good light.

But today it was arid in NYC, which was unusual for a city surrounded by water. New York in deep summer was steamy, but today the mercury hovered at ninety-nine, and a south wind had ripped away much of the moisture. The weather triggered memories of Kabul and how it was dry enough to suck the air out of your lungs. This was not a good start to the day, and he was glad that he dressed only in jeans and a tee. As he waited for the train, he ran his hand through his hair, forgetting that after hearing the day's weather report he had shaved his short hair down to a buzz. It was almost automatic, and when he gazed at the result in his bathroom mirror, he realized it was a mistake. He looked too much like the soldier he used to be and not like the undercover investigator he was.

Callum's jaw tightened, and his right hand formed a fist as he lowered it from his head. Buzzcut was a style, not an announcement he was law enforcement. He rubbed his hand on his chin to check his stubble. That wouldn't give him away as a cop. And then Callum shook his head. The person he would meet already knew he was a cop. And a buddy from prep school. He and Aaron Stirling had been tight before the 2008 crash dashed Aaron's Harvard hopes. Callum, via his trust fund, had no such problems, and their paths diverged.

Lost in his thoughts, he almost missed his stop at the 96th Street station, the demarcation line between wealth and poverty in NYC. He pushed out of the car and onto the underground platform, automatically swiveling his head to scope out threats.

*Relax, Reilly*, he scolded himself. *This is not Kabul.*

But an unyielding bump of hard metal from behind got his heart pumping. Callum whirled to meet the person who invaded his personal space. His eyes widened when he saw it was an elderly woman with a walker trying to get onto the train.

"Young man," she said. "Can you move your ass? It's hard enough getting around." Callum swallowed hard. Had he not stopped his first trained instincts, he would have swept her to the ground, which was far too dark an action to start the day.

"Sorry, ma'am," he said.

She smiled. "It's a cute ass, though. In fact, with that copper top of yours, you kind of look like that adorable English prince with hair. So, I guess I'm not too upset." The woman winked at Callum and climbed onto the train. Callum smiled back. It had been too long since any woman complimented his looks, so he'd take one from a stranger, even if she was older than his grandmother.

He strode the two blocks to Aaron's Yorktown apartment, which sat on the edge of the Upper East Side and Harlem. Aaron kept an Upper East Side address in case any of his wealthy clients found out where he lived. But the location gave a nod to economy to get the cheapest rent possible. Now, he and his new wife, Kristal, had moved to a larger apartment, and the lease on this one had three months on it. Aaron asked if Callum could help a guy out. Aaron could sublet to anyone, but he didn't want the hassle of someone turning into a deadbeat renter, and Callum, he knew, was no deadbeat.

*See? Kudos from everyone,* he told himself. *An elderly woman thinks your ass is cute, and your former best friend thinks you aren't a deadbeat. Props for holding that rep up.*

The owners had painted the former red brick building a sunny yellow, and small oaks lined the sidewalk at regular intervals. Two young women—nannies—pushed baby carriages, and an older woman walked a well-groomed Shih-Tzu.

Callum found the inside foyer clean, with the brass mailboxes on the left brightly polished.

He pressed the buzzer and waited.

"Who is it?" a feminine voice asked.

"I'm sorry. I'm looking for Aaron Stirling's apartment. I'm supposed to see it?"

"Oh, the cop," the voice said. Her disparaging tone signaled that she didn't appreciate law enforcement. "Yeah, Aaron's at work. He asked me to show it. Come up."

Callum yanked the door at the first buzz. As expected, the unknown woman didn't hit the button for long.

The oak staircase wafted the aroma of lemon oil, and the hexagonal tiles, a hallmark of the building's age, shone as if waxed. Whoever took care of this building did so with love, and he understood why Aaron, who had a love of luxury, had rented here.

Again, there was no elevator, a sign of the building's age, but Callum didn't mind. He didn't hit the gym as often as he should, but the climb to the fourth floor was a breeze, not an inconvenience. Despite his initial rejection of the suggestion, he found that he might consider moving here.

*Besides, Callum, this is one step to getting in closer with Ianucci's social circle.*

He pressed the doorbell at the right-hand side of the door and waited.

After five long seconds, the door jerked open, and Callum's eyes widened. He had met this woman several times.

Heather Skye stood at the door while yanking a boot on her left foot. She wore skin-tight leather pants and a black lacy sleeveless tee that left little to the imagination. The tips of her glossy black hair shone a bright magenta, and she wore a nose ring and a lip piercing. Heather looked wild and hot and was just the type of woman that could get a man's fire roaring, except for the frosty glare that she shot him.

"What the hell are you looking at?" she said.

*Sex on a stick.*

*Check that, Reilly. You're here for business, not play.*

"I'm just here to look at the apartment, ma'am."

Her head snapped up and gave him a long, appraising glance as if measuring every part of him. The intensity of the gaze made him shiver, and he didn't know why. It was as if when he addressed her as ma'am, a lightbulb switched on inside her, and she focused her attention on him like a 90,000-lumen tactical flashlight.

"Ma'am? But you're not a Southern boy, are you?"

"No, ma'am. Ex-military."

"A cop and ex-military," she huffed. "Well, I should have guessed."

Callum had no idea why she should be able to guess, but then figuring out the ins and outs of Miss Heather Skye was not today's mission.

She cocked her head. "But I suppose I should thank you since you helped Kristal when you arrested her. You made it possible that she didn't need to spend a night in jail, and I appreciate it. That woman is as close as blood to me. So come in. Don't mind the mess. I'm moving into a new apartment myself, and I'm just staying here until the super paints it."

"Mess" was an understatement. Callum entered the apartment. A clothes-covered couch sat to his right. A red brick wall stretched the length of the residence into the prominent kitchen area. It stood separate from the living area only because a granite counter, covered with left-over takeout boxes, jutted from the brick wall. The kitchen's cherry-stained cabinets and stainless appliances lent an upscale air to the small apartment, even if dishes flowed over the top of the sink. But this was New York, and if you could find rent for an affordable price, it would be what most Americans considered tiny.

But the apartment's disarray made his mouth twitch, and his Marine-primed thinking processes devised a plan of attack for demolishing the litter.

*Not your barrel. Not your monkeys.*

"I understand there is a bedroom?"

"Sure, through that door." Heather waved her hand to a closed door, and he pushed it open.

The bedroom was in no better shape than what he'd seen through the rest of the apartment. The bedclothes lay thoroughly wrecked, as if Heather'd had different men in her bed, sharing her hospitality. The bathroom off the bedroom needed several good scrubbings.

He turned back to the door to find Heather leaning against the doorjamb, studying him.

"You inspect everything, don't you?"

"I'm a detective, so yes."

She shook her head. "No. It's more than that. Well, the rent is $2,500 a month."

"Aaron told me," he said, peeking into a closet. "And when are you leaving?"

"By the end of the week. But don't worry, I'll clean it. But you're pretty cool about the rent, and on a New York City detective's salary, I wouldn't take you for an Upper East Side guy."

He shrugged. "I told Aaron I'd look at it, so I am. I can make do for a few months until I find my place."

"For a guy that's been in New York for a year, you're not settled in."

"Real estate market is tough," he said coolly. "Haven't found a place I like yet. What about your apartment?"

"Is that your way of asking me where I used to live?"

"No. I know." He tapped his head. "Photographic memory. I have your address from when I did the paperwork when I arrested your roommate."

"That was a year ago. Someone rented it already. Besides, an Upper East Side guy like yourself wouldn't like it. It's too small."

"Smaller than this?"

"The bathroom was so small the toilet was in the shower."

"You're pulling my leg."

She chuckled. "I'm not. Here." She picked up a purse from the floor and pulled out her phone. Heather studied the screen as she thumbed through her photos. "Take a gander," she said. He stared at the picture, and it displayed a toilet sitting in the shower, with the hose from the handheld shower snaking a trail on the wall.

"Gives a new meaning to the word 'bidet,'" he said dryly.

She laughed. "That's one big honking bidet, for sure. I loved the pulse action on that shower head. Brought me many happy moments."

"Yeah, I'm sure you flooded the toilet with those happy moments."

She chuckled. "You're naughty. I like that in a man."

"Not so much."

"Aw, poor Mr. Detective doesn't get much attention from the ladies. Or is it men?" She tilted her head and smiled.

"It's none of your business," he said too roughly.

She stood straight, and her demeanor changed from joking to disapproving. He found that he liked the stern look on her face, like a librarian catching someone fooling around in the stacks. Her bright red lips pursed, and her green eyes narrowed. He found her unappeasable attitude pinged a part of him long ignored. All she needed was a pair of black horned-rimmed glasses, and he could show her what wrecking the sheets meant.

*You're here for work, not play.*

His nose itched as he glanced at her.

"Say, that wedding of Aaron and Kristal's was quite something."

"Yeah, they practiced for months to get it right. They wrote the vows themselves except for the collaring ceremony. That's standard stuff."

"I didn't understand the collaring thing."

"I don't suppose you would," she said. Heather gazed at him again with that piercing intensity that got under his skin. She held out her hand.

"Phone, please."

He handed it back.

"Good boy," she said as if praising him.

This was too weird. Callum didn't like the predatory look in her eye, or how she seemed to get some perverse amusement trying to rattle him. "I have to get going," he said. "I'm meeting up with Aaron and some of his friends. I guess their wives are doing a girls' night out."

Heather settled her bag on her shoulder and fished for something under a pile of clothes. She pulled out a pink-wrapped box with a sparkly ribbon.

"Yeah. I know. I'm going," Heather said. "And by the way it's not a girls' night out. It's a baby shower for Lexi. But you guys will play poker. Have fun. Make sure to lock the door when you leave."

And with that, Miss Heather Skye walked out of the apartment, leaving him to wonder what just happened.

# 2

"I'm sorry I'm late," Heather said as Lexi Cashman flung open the door. The baby shower's guest of honor threw her arms around Heather's neck and hugged her. Heather awkwardly juggled the wrapped gift she'd brought, what with Lexi's prominent baby bump.

"Thanks so much for coming," Lexi gushed.

Lexi was the happiest Heather had ever seen her, but why wouldn't the luckiest of lucky gals not be ecstatic? She had a fabulously handsome and rich husband, a gorgeous Fifth Avenue apartment, and a beautiful baby on board.

*Ow, Heather Skye. Are you a touch jealous?*

Heather, being scrupulously honest, recognized who and what she was. Finding that mysterious one guy that made her burn with passion, and yet could hold up to the demands of a BDSM Domme had proved, so far, to be impossible.

*Am I asking too much?* she thought.

"Of course I would," Heather said. "Where do I put this?"

"I'll take that." Samantha Ianucci, Lexi's best friend, scooped the box out of Heather's hands. "There is food at the breakfast counter, and liquor at the bar. Help yourself to plenty of both."

"Is this Sean Cashman's place?" a voice behind her said, and Heather rolled her eyes. She glanced over her shoulder to find a tall, ginger hulk standing behind her with a bemused expression.

"Hi," Lexi said brightly.

*The woman could percolate coffee with her smile*, Heather thought.

Heather scoffed. "Yes, it is, and you know it. Have you been following me?"

"Only since the subway. You seemed to know where you were going, and I didn't mind the scenery."

Heather rolled her eyes again. *I know where you are going, buddy. Not home with me.*

"Lexi, you've met Detective Reilly. Cash invited him to the card game."

"Yes," she said. Lexi lifted her head to meet the detective's eyes. "Come in, the guys are in the second door to the right."

"Hey," Samantha protested, "that's my room."

"You never officially moved in, and since you've been with Master William, haven't slept here. I can't hold real estate forever, woman."

"Pshaw, there are six bedrooms in this behemoth."

"Just be glad we didn't choose it for the baby's bedroom. Then you'd have no place to go. I am not ripping out the gym to give you a place to lay your head."

Samantha laughed. "You are so bad, Lexi Winters Cashman. I can't wait to get the games started. Revenge will be sweet."

*Oh, dear Lord,* thought Heather. *One of those parties with silly games? And a diaper "cake"?* She hoped there was alcohol because she would need it.

Reilly looked up the hallway, looking unsure. Samantha swept her arm around his, and Heather's gut clenched.

*Why should you care if another woman touches him?*

She shouldn't, and Heather didn't understand her reaction.

Lexi took Heather's arm and steered her to the sunken living room in the middle of the circular open floor plan. On her left was a kitchen-bar counter packed with food. It peeked into a kitchen with granite counters and gigantic stainless-steel appliances. The entire room would swallow Kristal's and her old apartment. Walnut stained wood posts framing either side of the granite counter held accordion panels that could hide the kitchen from view. Inside the kitchen was Kristal with her back to the door.

"What are you doing?"

With surprise on her face, she whirled. Heather eyed a chocolate smudge on Kristal's cheek.

"Shoo. Return to the living room. I'm preparing a game."

"What on earth would that be?"

"You'll see. Go." Kristal gave her a fierce glance.

"No, show me now." Heather elbowed closer to her partner-in-crime, and her eyes widened. She looked down on six small babies. Kristal had a small ice cream scoop in her hand filled with chocolate frosting.

"What the hell?"

"Isn't it the cutest thing? Marzipan makes up the babies, and I'm putting the chocolate frosting in their diapers. We made the diapers from rolled-out marshmallows."

"Are you out of your mind, Kristal Stirling?"

Kristal giggled.

"What are you laughing about?"

"I still can't get over 'Kristal Stirling.' Rich, huh?" Kristal picked up a glass baby bottle and drank from it.

Heather stared at her in shock. "What are you drinking?"

"Wine, of course. Well, a wine cooler."

Heather gazed at the bottle, and the candy babies with marshmallow diapers with chocolate frosting in them and her best friend drinking a wine cooler out of a baby bottle. The world tilted, and she felt dizzy.

"You are insane."

"Oh, relax, Heather. It's a party."

"Kristal, I've been walking on the weird side of life for all these many years, and this is the strangest thing I've ever seen."

"I think it's cute. Samantha went through a lot to pull this party together for her best friend, and—" Kristal stopped and swallowed hard.

"What, Kristal?"

Kristal pursed her lips. "Nothing."

"Tell me, Kristal. What's on your mind?"

Kristal's jaw set, and she stared at the marzipan babies. "I would hope that my best friend would go through the trouble for me."

Heather's eyes widened, and she glanced at the wine cooler baby bottle again.

"You're not—"

"No," Kristal said firmly. "But Aaron and I have been talking, and well, we're thinking about it. I like spending time with Mitch, Sheila, and their two kids. It's fun."

"Fun?" Heather said. Mitch was Aaron's best friend, and it was only natural that Aaron and Kristal spend time with them. But having a child? Her stomach roiled at the thought of crying rugrats, and chocolate-frosting-filled diapers, and her best friend having less time for her than she did now. The earth fell away, and her heels wobbled under her feet.

*Stop this, Heather Skye. Your friend's life changed for the better. You should be happy for her.*

"I am, I am," Heather muttered.

"What?" Kristal said.

"Nothing," demurred Heather. This party was a bad idea. It triggered too many things she'd buried under her leather and her indomitable will. But she couldn't leave gracefully. Kristal, Lexi, and Samantha were all part of *La Corda Rosa*—a central part of Heather's life. All she could do was grin and get through this even if the next two hours tortured her.

"Let's get started," Samantha called from the next room.

"Just a minute," Kristal called back. She didn't look at Heather, as her best friend finished her task by pulling up and twisting the ties of the last baby's diaper.

"Hey," Heather said. "You know when the time comes, we'll have a ginormous, honking party. Nothing would make me happier than to give it for you. I haven't mentioned it because I didn't want to ruin the surprise."

A small smile crooked the corner of Kristal's lips.

"And I suppose you'll tell me that you have the hotel room already booked."

"Yep. And I've ordered the strippers. Male, of course, jumping out of a cake, all wearing diapers with chocolate frosting in them so we can lick—"

"I think you have the wrong party," Kristal said with a chuckle. "And you have the dirtiest mind."

Heather sighed. *Not lately.*

"What? There is nothing wrong with a little diaper play. Some guys get off on it."

"Sometimes, I wonder what you did with clients when you were a professional dominatrix."

*Sometimes I do too.*

"Ladies," Samantha singsonged. "We can't start without you."

"These little guys are ready. Let's go join the party."

Heather glanced at the candy babies with their little diapers filled with chocolate frosting leaking out of the sides.

"And what will we do with these?"

Kristal laughed. "You'll see. It will be fun.

Heather and Kristal settled in on the curved white leather sofa that dominated the sunken living room with Sheila—Mitch's wife—and Lexi. It was a small party, but as Heather had explained, it was more to raise Lexi's spirits as she got closer to the big day. Even though Lexi smiled a broad grin, Heather could imagine her anxiety. She herself had experienced the fears and nervousness about giving birth once long ago. Again, and to her dismay, Heather felt a pang of envy as she glanced at the smiling women around her. She had no such support ten years ago when she was young, frightened, and alone.

Samantha produced a tray of baby bottle drinks and a bowl of ice cubes.

"Now, as our icebreaker, we're playing a little game of 'waiting for baby.' In the ice cubes are tiny babies just waiting to arrive. The first one whose ice cube melts yells out, 'I have a baby,' and wins a $100 gift certificate to any Romallo's Restaurant, courtesy of Master William Ianucci."

"Ooh, that's a great prize," Lexi said.

Samantha darted to stand in front of Heather with the tray of baby bottle drinks and ice cubes, and Heather glimpsed the frozen babies in the ice cubes. She shivered at a memory she didn't want to re-experience and shook her head.

"I'm good," she said.

"But—"

"Excuse me," she said. "I need the ladies'."

"Third door on the right." Samantha sounded confused, but Heather couldn't explain. She had to escape.

"Thanks," Heather said.

She didn't remember getting to the bathroom. All she knew was that her knees wouldn't hold her up. Heather sat on the toilet and buried her face in her hands. Why did she come here? Why did she think she could handle a nice, normal baby shower when she was anything but a nice, normal woman?

There were no tears. They'd been cried out a decade ago. But there was a fiery ache in her throat that came from wanting to cry tears long spent. She couldn't change what happened. Nothing could. And she wasn't at fault.

*Yeah, Heather Skye, that's why you changed your name, ran away, and never looked back.*

A knock at the bathroom door caused Heather to jerk her head up.

"Occupied," she said.

"I've been waiting fifteen minutes here," said a rough male voice. It was Reilly. "I wouldn't complain, but things are getting a little urgent here."

If this were a BDSM game, she would have told him to hold it, then bend over so she could swat his butt while he winced at his ass reddened while needing to relieve himself. She'd watch him squirm and listen to him whimper while she enjoyed the man's allowing this torture for her pleasure.

*Why do I conjure up thoughts like this?*

*Because it's fun.*

*But is it?*

"Hey?"

Heather shook her head, and fortified with annoyance, stood and crossed the bathroom, again more massive than her apartment, and yanked the door open.

"Can a woman not have some peace?" she said sharply.

Reilly's eyes glittered as they raked her body. His fiery gaze examined every single inch of her body with a sizzling glare, communicating what he wanted.

*Too bad, Big Red,* she thought. *That's not how it works for me because vanilla is not my favorite flavor. But Big Red is the perfect pet name for you.*

The detective edged closer to her, and an electric spark popped between their bodies.

*Relax, Heather Skye. It's just from the carpet underneath your feet.*

Only, she glanced down and realized that marble tiled the bathroom floor, and hardwood lay under his.

She sucked in a breath and looked up again, then found she could not tear her eyes away from his.

Her heart raced, but she drew on her years of Domme experience to keep her expression ultra-cool and disinterested. But deep down in a place Heather did not examine often she recognized, much like when prey knows a predator stalks them, that this man was pure danger.

Reilly was opening his mouth to say something when Kristal showed up behind him.

"Hey. You've missed the best games. Come on. We're cutting the cake."

Heather squeezed past Reilly without letting a single inch of her skin touch his. She dared not because she suspected that once she did, she wouldn't stop.

# 3

Heather pushed past his body, and his dick swelled uncomfortably in his slacks. Callum thought if he took one step, he'd explode.

*Jesus, Reilly, you aren't a teenager.*

The women sauntered down the hall, with Heather clutching the other woman's arm. He couldn't help but notice Heather's round butt swaying in those tight leather pants as she took graceful steps on her stiletto heels.

Unconsciously, Callum licked his lips even as his throat felt desert dry.

*To get a taste of that*, he thought.

His head swam, and he had to get out of this hallway. He stumbled into the bathroom and shut and locked the door. He did not need to get interrupted.

*Your problem, Cal, old friend, is that you haven't dated in forever. Now you see sex-on-a-stick, and all you want to do is gobble it down.*

But after reaching the toilet, and unzipping his pants, his hard dick wouldn't allow him to relieve the fullness in his kidneys. Cal needed to wait until he settled down or—

Damn it. Heather's butt cheeks swaying in those tight black

leathers of hers made his heart race. One, two, and a third pull on his dick, and he was harder than he'd been in forever. Heather's red, pouting lips, black magenta-tipped hair, the swell of her breasts peeking out of her low-cut sweater, the skin-tight leather pants, and the thigh-high stiletto boots commanded his thoughts.

His knees shook under him as his body exploded in fire.

"Fuuuck," he gasped as he spilled over his hand.

His breath ran ragged as he leaned against the wall with spend on his hands.

"Jesus," he swore under his breath. He never had that reaction to a woman before. Pleasant fantasies, yes, that edged him from desire to fulfillment, but never where his body shook.

He had to sit down, and he sank to the toilet. He reached for a hand towel sitting in a stack on the vanity counter and realized only after he wiped his hand that he'd leave a cum-smeared towel behind.

Hell. Callum came to this luxurious Fifth Avenue apartment to work, not cum, and his face burned with embarrassment at his schoolboy antics. People's lives were at stake. This investigation took a year too long to get close enough to his suspects to get a social invitation to a private party—even if it was the male half of a baby shower.

He had no illusions. His great poker playing skill did not net him the invite. He sucked at poker, something that a man did not admit, even to himself. No, this tight-knit group of men needed a fifth for poker. Callum's number came up since he'd brushed the edges of the group for the past year and perhaps seemed the safest of their near associates.

Little did they know. Callum had been a close friend of Aaron Stirling in the past, but no longer felt the bonds of friendship since he suspected Aaron was in deeper with this group than was good for him. Of the three, he was less likely involved, but people gauge you by the company you keep.

Cal shook his head at his juvenile behavior. He rinsed out the towel and wiped his sticky gunk from the walls, feeling like a criminal cleaning up a crime scene. What the hell was he thinking?

*You were thinking about Miss Heather Skye, you fool.*

He tossed the hand towel in a laundry hamper by the wall and returned to the card game. When he opened the door, a thick waft of piquant cigar smoke and the aroma of expensive whiskey greeted him.

"Where the hell have you been?" Aaron said.

Callum shrugged and sat at his seat, where he found an uncut cigar lying at his place at the table. He picked it up and sniffed and found it delectable.

"Thanks," he said to his host. Sean Cashman handed him a cigar cutter and a lighter.

Cashman owned the aviation company Cashman Industries, and his company produced jet engines. The company worked on prototypes for space shuttle engines, but lost a huge contract to another, more famous, contractor. His company, worth billions, had diversified to cover the shock of aviation losses, which only seemed to rack up over time. However, the space shuttle engines were a particular dream of Cashman's, and losing the contract had to hurt. It might be a motive to get back at his country.

Callum cut the end and put the cigar in his mouth without lighting it. He was content to do this. Smoking cigars relaxed him too much, and he did not need to get more relaxed right now.

Miss Heather took care of that in absentia.

Aaron slid into the chair on Callum's left. Another man, sitting next to Callum's right, who had curly red hair, picked up the lighter and held it to the cigar. Jaime Wilder was the lawyer for Sean Cashman. He was also the lawyer for William Ianucci, the dark-haired Italian on the other side of the table. Callum didn't dare wave it away. He wanted these men to think he was their friend.

Which he was not.

"Thanks, Wilder," he said.

"No problem," the lawyer said.

Callum checked out his chips, which captured most of his buy-in, and glanced at the table at the other stacks. Ianucci's remained about the same, Wilder's was a bit depleted, and Sean's seemed to have an extra stack or two.

"What are we playing?" Callum said.

"Let's do some Texan Hold 'Em," Ianucci said.

"Sure," Callum said, and Wilder and Cashman agreed.

"What are the girls doing out there?" Ianucci said. He glanced at Callum.

"Didn't check it out."

"What the hell took you so long?" Cashman said.

"Waiting for the bathroom," Callum said.

Cashman gave a disbelieving glance at Callum. "You should have said something, Reilly. I have like six bathrooms in this place."

"I figured, but I didn't want to go searching through your house." *Not without a warrant.*

That would be awkward to explain in court.

*Your honor, I was looking for a bathroom in this Fifth Avenue condo. I just stumbled upon financial records showing Mr. Cashman fronted money-laundering activities for the Ianucci crime family and the Red Talon terrorist group.*

*And what were you doing in Mr. Cashman's condo without a warrant?*

*Playing poker for stakes is illegal, I know, but hey, you gotta do what you must.*

Yeah. Right.

Cashman scoffed as Ianucci dealt the river cards. "Right. I've seen how you look at Heather."

Cal took the cards Ianucci dealt and spread them in his hand. The three did nothing for him.

"I don't know what you're talking about."

The three men laughed.

"She's not in your league anyway," Wilder said. "I'll take two cards." He slid two cards toward Ianucci.

"What do you mean?" Callum picked up his glass to sip his whiskey.

Ianucci pitched Wilder his cards. Cashman stood pat. "Miss Heather has been part of the BDSM scene for a long time. She used to be a professional Domme before she and Miss Kristal opened Store BIO."

Callum almost spat his whiskey back in his glass but held it in. The liquor burned like liquid fire as it went down.

He held back a cough when he spoke. "You mean—"

"I said Domme, not a prostitute. There is a difference," Ianucci said. Disdain dripped from his words.

"Here," Cashman said. "I'll top off your whiskey. And no offense, you're a good guy. But Heather Skye likes a different type of man than you."

He was afraid to ask, but Callum had to know.

"What type of man is that?"

"Someone who'll kiss her feet," smirked Wilder.

*I could do that.* To his surprise, he liked the idea. He bet she had gorgeous feet inside those spike-heeled boots.

"Someone who likes pain with his pleasure," Cashman said.

Again, Cal thought that might be fun.

"He's not getting the picture, guys. Heather likes submissive men."

"And that," Aaron said, "is a whole different mindset."

"And you would know that how?"

Aaron half-chuckled. "Kristal thought I was submissive when I first met her."

"And why did she think that?"

"He told her." Cashman laughed. "Our boy Aaron here wanted to date her so bad that he was willing to tell her anything."

The other men laughed.

"Hey," Aaron said. "In my defense, it worked in the short term."

Ianucci took his cigar from his mouth and pointed it at Aaron. "And you almost lost her for it, too."

"True. But we got it straightened out."

"I saw," Callum said. "I mean, that wedding ceremony at *La Corda Rosa* was something else."

The image of Aaron tying Heather in an intricate weave of red rope and suspending her from the ceiling burned in his memory. Still, he couldn't reconcile doing any of that to a woman. Why would she like it? Why would Aaron? That's the thing that made Callum think differently of his friend. Aaron, when Callum first met him, was as straight an arrow as anyone could be.

"That rope suspension took months of training to get right," Ianucci said.

Now there was a guy that Callum could imagine tying up women for fun.

"Yes," Aaron agreed. "But it lost me Heather's nickname of Vanilla Ice."

Callum's four companions laughed again.

"Heather called you that?" Callum said. After Aaron's and

Kristal's wedding, he didn't think anyone would call Aaron "vanilla."

"So what do you think, William? Is Samantha the next one the gals will have a baby shower for?"

"Oh, we've discussed it. It's no secret what I want. I imagine once Samantha holds Lexi's baby, she won't be content until she has one of her own. She's too worried about Lexi to think about it."

"Worried," Wilder said with a frown. "Is there a reason to?"

Cashman shrugged. "Not that I know of, but you know—"

A knock on the door interrupted the conversation. Samantha poked her head in. "Come on, guys. There is one last game we need Cash's input on. Put those cards and those nasty cigars down and come help us."

Callum could see that he was getting nowhere here. It was all baby and wife talk, hardly conducive to organized gang chatter.

"Maybe I should leave," Callum said.

"Oh, no," Cash said. "Not until the women break up this shindig. Once one of you leaves, the other will find excuses, so you're all hanging around. I will not be the last man here among the women. You're taking yours home with you."

"But I don't have a wife," Wilder said. "You, Ianucci, scooped up the best one."

"Not my problem I'm so irresistible," Ianucci said. His friends continued to rib him as they left the room.

Callum hung back as the men made their way to the living room. Despite the men's back-talk, Cash, Ianucci, and Aaron seemed happy to rejoin their wives. As bachelors, he and Wilder stood by the food and watched as the women fussed over their husbands as they settled in on the enormous couch.

"Okay," Samantha said. "The next and last game is 'who said this?' with a twist. Now I've spent tons of time gathering the intel for this game, so I can't play. The twist is I have a question and answer from each husband and wife in here. The first one of you to answer correctly gets one of these lovely parting gifts. There are a bunch of gift cards here, and you'll get a chance to pick out of the basket which one. And one of these cards has a lovely spa weekend on Martha's Vineyard, courtesy of our host, Sean Cashman."

Callum watched as Heather excused herself and surreptitiously made for the front door and he thought she had the right idea.

"See you later, man," he said to Wilder, who gave him a nod as he watched the game.

He slipped out and grabbed the door before it closed. In the elevator, he smiled at her while she ignored him.

"Going home?" he said.

She shook her head.

"Want to share a cab?"

Heather stared straight ahead as the elevator descended. When it stopped, she tossed him an authoritative yet sexy glance that made him shiver.

"Listen, Big Red, stop right there before you get in over your head. You are as vanilla as they come, and that's not me. So whatever ideas are percolating in your head, shut them off now."

She walked out of the elevator, and Callum had one thought. He wanted to press her luscious body against him and kiss the anger from her eyes.

But how could he get close enough to do that?

## 4

Heather stood at the cash register of Store BIO and slammed the quarters into their slot hard enough for one to jump out and land on the floor. When she bent down to retrieve it, she hit her head underneath the register drawer.

"Ouch! Godless piece of crap machinery," she spat. Pain spread through the back of her head.

She stood while rubbing the sore spot with her fingers and examined the drawer for damage or blood. She saw neither, but that did nothing to ease the pique in her soul.

Kristal was late for work—again. At first, Heather excused Kristal's tardiness because she was a newlywed. There were just things a newly married couple needed when they were in love and discovering married life, such as couple time. And Heather loved her best friend to pieces. But standing alone in the store that they started together one more morning was too much to take.

Hell, maybe she was getting close to her monthly. That was always good for a few days of high emotion. But she checked the calendar on her smartphone, and no, she had another week before she started the roller-coaster before the actual event.

No. Heather had another problem, and it was she hadn't had a boyfriend in forever.

Yesterday's baby shower only compounded her angst. She couldn't blame the women. They had their princes and their happily-ever-afters and she was glad for them. But she couldn't help the sense that life wasn't just passing her by. It marched by like a thirty-piece marching band.

The buzzer rang, and she glanced at the appointment book to find no one scheduled. A drop-in? Those were rare.

There was a reason why they called the store By Invitation Only.

A peek through the peephole made her mouth quirk. What the hell was the Big Red doing here?

She yanked open the door and put her left hand on the doorjamb and the other on her hip. Sure, this position maximized the swell of her breasts under the magenta leather vest she wore today, but that's not why she leaned into the jamb. No. She'd let Big Red know that he wasn't welcome here at the store.

Now if she could only get the moisture in her panties to say the same thing. She needed to have a serious talk with her woman parts.

"Detective," she said.

His eyes raked her as if he gazed at a dessert cart.

*Oh, no, Mr. Detective Man. I am not on your menu.*

"Miss Skye, may I come in?" Reilly said. His voice sounded a little thick, but New York City air had that effect on some people.

"Did you get an invitation to shop here?" she said.

"I need an invitation to shop this store?" Reilly said with surprise.

"Yes."

"That's weird."

"It's what we do. We don't need a bunch of people not involved in the lifestyle traipsing through."

"The BDSM lifestyle," he said.

"Correct."

"I'm not exactly a newbie," he said.

Heather had to restrain a chuckle. His whole demeanor, such as his wide eyes as he tried to peek past her, screamed to her that he had no clue about the lifestyle.

She waved her hand. "Well, come right in. What are you looking for?"

She stepped away from the door and waited until he walked past her before she let the door shut. Since it was a heavy glass door, it closed with a thud. For effect, she set the security alarm.

"You locked the door? Isn't that against local fire codes?"

"The door automatically unlocks in case of a fire alarm," Heather said. She moved toward the display of BDSM implements on the first row of the free-standing wire wall of display racks. She plucked a flogger from the wall and struck her palm with it.

At the sound of the flogger hitting her flesh, he whirled.

"What are you doing?"

She was well aware of the usual response she got with her skin-tight leather wardrobe, her long magenta nails matching the ends of her hair, and thigh-high boots. A submissive man would quake in his shoes. Someone with a Dom mindset would give her a smoldering stare.

He gave her the stare. And his piercing gaze reached into her soul, and he examined everything about her with that one gaze. But that was impossible. Of course, he was a detective and was probably excellent at his job. He came through for Kristal when he didn't need to.

*Maybe you found the rare good guy.*

"Me?" she said with a touch of innocence in her voice. She slapped her hand again with the flogger. "Just waiting on the customer. What can I do for you today, Detective?"

Reilly turned on his heel, taking in the store in one sweep.

"I heard you were a professional Domme?"

Who told him that? She figured that Reilly was attempting to knock her off-center. It was a cop's trick, and she didn't appreciate it.

"Oh? Are you looking for a Domme?" Heather let the words out in a silky-smooth tone she found particularly effective.

"No," he said. "I was just asking—"

She returned the flogger to its wire peg on the display, bending forward to show off her butt in her tight leather pants. Reilly stopped speaking. She imagined his eyes growing wider, or maybe some drool at the corner of his mouth. She smiled at her brief fantasy.

*Hey. If you can't have fun at work, it's no fun at all.*

She turned crisply on her spiked heel and smiled. Heather didn't see drool at the corner of his mouth, but she spotted lust in his eyes.

"Well, Detective, either you shop, or you leave. I'm a busy woman and have a ton of work to do."

"I don't see any other customers."

"Most of what this shop sells is custom leatherwork from private orders. These," and she swept her arm to indicate the other merchandise, "are add-on sales."

He picked up a GIMP mask with detachable eye patches and a mouth gag. He eyed it with curiosity.

"People buy something like this?"

"Oh, come now, Detective," she said. She oozed seduction in her voice. "You're a big boy. You've seen nothing like it in the porn you watch?"

He shook his head. "Not my thing."

"But you said you weren't a newbie at BDSM."

"I'm a man of action," said Reilly.

Good comeback. Heather admired a man good with words.

His gaze landed with curiosity on the merchandise. Heather saw the detective had no clue about real BDSM.

"Well," she said. "What holds your interest? Masks?"

"There are a lot of animal masks." He narrowed his eyes as he examined the kitten, bunny, and fox masks on the side rear counter on the left of the entrance to the back room.

Heather smiled a huge grin.

"Is that your kink? Pet fetish?"

"I didn't say—"

"I have a lovely collection of tails to go with any mask."

"Tails?" Now his eyebrows scrunched up even more as if contemplating a quadratic equation.

"They come in different plug sizes and even with remote-controlled vibrators for you and your play partner's pleasure."

"Plugs? You mean butt plugs?"

"Well, of course," Heather said. She edged closer with slow, sensual movements that emphasized her lithe body. His Adam's apple bobbed as he swallowed hard, and he backed away. He bumped into the counter, jiggling the masks on their display forms, and jumped when one with tiny bells chimed.

"What the hell?"

"Hell? Oh, no. Shop BIO is all about pleasure. What's yours, Detective?" She smiled at him again and lowered her eyes. Heather glanced at him through her eyelashes, which she found was a surefire way to tickle a man's sex bone. And boy, did Heather do that. The bulge in his pants had grown noticeable since he entered the store and now strained against his jeans. She almost licked her lips at the sight but stopped before she did.

*What is wrong with you, Heather Skye?*

"You're pranking me," he accused. Heather found the heat in his eyes sexy.

*A little danger with your pleasure, Miss Skye?*

"Me?" She spoke with total innocence in her voice. "I'm just trying to determine my customer's *needs*. What are your *needs*, Detective Reilly?"

Reilly straightened and crossed his arms and glared at her.

"Maybe, I need to whip a bad girl's ass to get her to behave."

"Hmmm," Heather said approvingly. "I have a wonderful collection of floggers just for that. Or perhaps a nice riding crop? Crops have such a lovely sting."

"And you would know all about that," he said darkly.

This was getting better and better.

"Of course I do," she said. "It is my business."

She turned and pulled a riding crop from the same display.

"Hold out your hand," she said.

"What?"

"Just do it," she said. Heather added the edge of command to her voice that had been so effective with her former clients, and hesitantly Reilly offered his hand.

With a swift jerk of her arm, she expertly landed the quirt's end on Reilly's palm.

"Ouch," he said. The detective yanked his hand away. "What did you do that for?"

"I'm demonstrating its sting. A serviceable keeper won't leave a mark, but it communicates the business at hand nicely."

"Keeper?" he said.

"Now, you're teasing me, Detective. As a practiced BDSM hand, you know the keeper is the flat business end of the crop. Shall I give you a practical demonstration?" She leaned forward to the counter to push out her rear and handed the crop to him.

With a light in his eyes, he snatched it from her hand.

"You want me to strike you?" he said. His voice dripped pure gravel wrapped in fire.

"Please. I want my customers perfectly satisfied with their selections."

"Well, if you want it."

Reilly struck with a ferocity that Heather did not expect. Pain shot through her in a shock wave and receded to pleasurable tingles that ran through her body.

"I can see that you've had practice," she said.

She turned her head to see Reilly's face turn pure red. He started at the crop and looked into her eyes. Callum released the quirt and allowed it to fall to the floor.

"I have to go," he said hoarsely.

Heather almost made a snarky remark but caught a haunted expression in his eyes. She blinked and realized she'd gone too far in her teasing. She opened her mouth to apologize. It was irresponsible of her to engage in play without knowing his triggers.

"No. I really must go. Goodbye."

With that, Reilly strode to the door and yanked at it. He whirled and glared at her.

"Unlock this thing and let me out of here."

"Sure," she said sincerely. She walked behind the counter and pressed the door release button. Reilly jerked the door open with such force the display window on the right side shook. He strode through the opening as if Heather had committed a grave offense.

"What was that about?"

She jumped and turned to see her business partner Kristal standing in the entrance that joined Heather's workroom and the store.

"Fucking hell," complained Heather. "You don't need to sneak up on a woman."

"Sneak? With those supersonic ears of yours, you usually hear me even if I tiptoe in. Someone must have had your attention."

"Shut up," Heather said, too abruptly. "I was just showing

him the merchandise."

Kristal smirked. "I'm sure you were."

"Stop that."

"What?" Kristal said with innocence. The damned woman had picked up Heather's best moves.

"He was here for, for—"

Kristal gave her a skeptical glance.

"Well, I don't know why he was here. The conversation took a weird turn."

Kristal bent and retrieved the riding crop from the floor.

"Must have been very weird for it to register in the Heather Skye universe."

Heather stuck her tongue out at Kristal.

"Was he any good?"

Heather huffed in indignation. "You are the worst best friend ever."

Kristal winced. "What I'm about to say will cement that. But the good news is that in eight months I get to call you aunty!"

## 5

Reilly took quick strides from Store BIO, bewildered after striking Heather with the riding crop. His feet wobbled unsteadily under him, which was ridiculous. Hell, the rigors of war had tested Reilly, and he never let that shake him.

But one skirmish with Miss Heather Skye knocked him off his feet. He didn't know what to make of the smirk that came over her face when he planted the crop on her rear packed into her skin-tight leather pants. Reilly's hand buzzed from the kinetic energy that traveled the length of the quirt into his palm. For a second, he imagined delivering more than one stroke to Heather's willing ass, but he shoved that thought down. Men did not strike women, ever. Reilly was a soldier but he wasn't a sadist.

He decided the woman had a witchy ability to push buttons. The knowingness in her eyes, as if she discovered a secret well of kink inside Reilly's soul, alarmed him. But Reilly had seen enough of the wickedness of men to understand people projected their faults on others. No. He did not enjoy striking Miss Heather Skye with a riding crop.

But he did. His cock, already mutinously hard, throbbed at the electricity that shot through his body with that blow. And it stunned him.

He decided not to agonize over the encounter. Because of his job, he hadn't had a date in years. He got too close to the delectable Miss Skye, who zeroed in on his buttons. She stood as a walking porn fantasy in her magenta corset, leather pants, and thigh-high stiletto boots, a costume she cultivated probably to market her store.

Besides, she was a member of Ianucci's BDSM club, *La Corda Rosa*, which was Reilly's focus in his investigation. He admitted the idea tempted him to "cross the streams," and date her to gain entry into that circle more quickly. But he'd recently made inroads to infiltrate the Ianucci circle and he was glad he didn't pull the stunt of dating Heather. Her store was a perfect front for money laundering. After all, how would a former Domme get the money to open a store in the middle of Manhattan? Just because Ianucci opened new stores in his Italian food chain didn't limit his ability to sink cash into her store.

Maybe he needed to get upfront and personal with Heather to dig into that background.

His phone rang, and he found it was from Sergeant Frank Holtz

"Hello, Frank," he said.

"Reilly, how's your investigation going?"

"I'm getting closer."

Holtz was no dummy, and he spoke bluntly. "But no closer to actionable info."

"Well, I got invited to a social event with Ianucci and his circle. Plus, he invited me to his club to 'check out the action.'"

"But you have no evidence of Ianucci committing a crime."

Reilly winced. "No, Sergeant, I don't."

"Let's face it. It was a good lead, but it was a dead end. Wrap things up, and we'll point you in a better direction."

Reilly's stomach soured. Ending this investigation meant thirteen months of work would be flushed into the sewer. And the hit to his career as the "undercover man who couldn't" would dog him until his retirement.

He was too young to retire.

"Sergeant, I feel I'm close."

"Reilly, you've been in New York for what? Thirteen months?"

"Sarge, undercover can last up to—"

"Reilly, put the pin back in. I'm tired of you solving cases for the NYPD on our dime. Wrap it. I'm sending the orders up the chain now. Say your goodbyes to Chi-town. It's time to move on."

Callum's heart sank as he realized Holtz had already spoken with Captain Watrous. The only bright spot was that if Holtz initiated the orders now, it would take at least two weeks to a month to get new ones.

"Sure, Sarge. What's my billet?"

"I'll send you your orders."

He didn't like that Holtz wouldn't tell him. Either Holtz didn't have the info, which was unlikely, or he thought Reilly would object.

"Wait, Sarge. If I'm changing my duty station, I'd like to request leave."

"Leave?" Holtz said. His voice conveyed suspicion.

"I came on this assignment without leave. I have the time."

"Fine," Holtz said. "One week."

"Two. I have two weeks of leave, at least."

Holtz muttered under his breath about Reilly's stubbornness.

"Two weeks. But this investigation is over."

"I understand. Thank you, Sarge."

Reilly pocketed his phone and sighed. He had four to six weeks to crack this case. Holtz nixed the operation, but Captain Watrous had a keen interest in taking down the Ianucci family. They had made their living in organized crime for at least four generations. While Reilly conducted this investigation, he was co-supervised by Watrous and Holtz. That was the agreement. While at the Chi-town precinct, Reilly remained obligated to follow Watrous's orders.

He hoped.

Callum rode the subway line that took him south toward his station house and then a quick walk to the precinct. Yesterday's New York heat had carried through today. Callum didn't mind the heat, but the humidity was a killer. He wondered if he still had a clean shirt in his desk as he walked the steps into the station house. The atrium held a long oak desk that ran parallel to the back wall. Being nearly two hundred years old, it held up well. The hardwood floor, however, had seen better days. The constant shuffling of human feet had worn away its shellac long ago. This had shocked Callum when he first arrived. In the pricey neighborhood where he grew up, hardwood floors gleamed with constant care. But the city of New York never had the money to fix the things that needed it.

He waved to the sergeant overseeing the front desk and made his way up the oak staircase. On the second floor, which housed the detectives, he entered the cluttered room and sat at his desk. Because of the nomadic nature of Callum's work, he rarely had a regular office. Now he found the idea of not having this one place that defined his position unsettling. Here he was, Callum Reilly, an NYC detective who had a sense of solidity that he didn't have in NCIS.

"Reilly!"

Captain Watrous stood at the doorway of his office just off

the detective's room, filled with outdated desks and nearly ancient computers.

"Yes, sir."

Callum entered Watrous' office, which was a smaller version of the detective room. Boxed case files filled every available wall, and nooks circled his desk like a wagon train. One forlorn oak chair sat before the captain's desk.

"What can I do for you, sir?"

Watrous looked from his computer screen to Callum and gave him a tight smile.

"I got a call from your boss."

"Yes, sir." Callum resisted the urge to stare at his hands, and he kept his gaze level. He expected that Watrous would dislike that call.

"He wants you on another detail."

"Yes, sir."

"What's your progress on the Ianucci investigation?"

"The guys who hang with Ianucci invited me to a poker game with Ianucci present. He invited me to his club tonight. Other than that, not much."

"I don't fault you. As I told you, the Ianuccis have worked with NYC organized crime families for four generations. New people moving into their orbit make them wary. I'd say you've done well. But now we have this situation to deal with your boss."

"My SSA, sir."

"I'll never get used to that."

Callum smiled. "I understand, sir. I just call him 'Sarge.'"

Watrous pursed his lips. "How much time do you have before you shove off?"

"A month on the inside, though two weeks of that should be for leave."

"As of today, I'm assigning your workload, except the Ianucci case, to the other detectives. I want your full attention on this while you are here. The NCIS agreed that I would supervise you while you were here and I will."

"I expected no less, sir."

"Good. And one other thing. And I hesitate to mention this because I haven't gotten the approval yet, but it helps to have a heads up."

"Sir?"

"Have you thought about leaving the service?"

"No. The Marines are my home. It's that way with a lot of guys who decide to make a career of it."

"I see. What if I were to offer you a position here? Give you a place to land permanently? You're a good detective, and I like how you've handled your cases."

"I thought the NYPD had a long list of detective candidates."

"We do. I agree this is an unusual offer. But you're an experienced investigator, and you've blended very well with the community policing we do here. I'd be a fool to let you go without at least making the offer."

"Thank you, sir. There is a difference in pay and benefits. Not to disrespect the NYPD, but I make more with the NCIS, though money isn't my only concern."

"There isn't much I can do about the pay, but I'd like you to consider the benefits of living full time in one place."

"I will, sir."

"Good. I like having you around, Reilly. And you calling me 'sir' every time doesn't hurt either."

Callum laughed. "I aim to please."

"Think about it. I must wait on the approval anyway, so don't make changes yet."

Watrous wrote something on a sticky note and handed it to Callum. It was an address in Little Italy.

"That's the address of Jimmy Mack's Smoke Shop. Jimmy

Mack used to supervise the numbers for Ianucci and Phil Pragaeno's operations, but no longer. What the fracas was, I have no clue. But if anyone has dirt to spill on the Ianuccis, he'd be the one to do it."

"Has anyone used him as a CI?"

"No."

"But he's still running numbers?"

"The man hasn't worked an honest day in his life. The smoke shop is a front for the bookie operation. If his parents didn't own the building, he couldn't keep the storefront open."

"Okay, I'll check it out."

"Take backup with you. Matheson knows the neighborhood. And take two uniforms, too. If you can keep it low-key, good. If not, bring Jimmy Mack in and book him."

"Will do, Captain."

Two hours later, with Detective Matheson and two uniforms in tow, they pulled in to Little Italy. They navigated the tiny streets clogged with traffic, legally parked cars, and illegally parked delivery trucks. One of the uniforms drove, and the other rode shotgun in the front seat. At their destination Callum and Matheson climbed from the back seat to stand before the storefront. Neon signs littered the large display panes of glass advertising different brands of cigars and cigarettes under a rounded green canopy. Inside appeared dark, but a sign on the front door said, "Open."

Callum glanced at Matheson, his erstwhile partner. Lean and dark-haired, Matheson came from a long line of New York City cops and wore the job with an offhanded sternness. The thirty-something man rarely smiled, and he appeared to survey every situation as if looking for the one thing that could do him harm. Callum appreciated Matheson's on-the-job attitude, and Callum thought he should cultivate more of it in himself. But having walked the streets of Kabul in a sixty-pound pack, carrying a ten-pound M27, it was hard to view New York streets as dangerous as that. Sure, Callum had to be cautious, but he didn't expect to walk on a tripwire or landmine in NYC.

A buzzer over the door announced Callum's arrival in the store. The lingering scents of tobacco, brewing coffee, and chewing gum hung in the air. A long display case ran the store's length on the left, while antique mahogany-stained magazine racks ran the right-hand length. Inside the locked glass display sat boxes of cigars, e-cigarettes, and vape mods. Tobacco, glass pipes, and hookahs tenanted other sections under the glass. A cigarette display hung off the counter, showing the logos of various brands of cigarettes.

But no one tended the front end of the store.

Matheson's mouth twitched, showing his dislike of the situation.

"Hello?" Callum called.

He glanced at Matheson, who frowned. He nodded his head toward a back door cracked open.

Callum advanced on the door with his hand on his gun inside his suit jacket. He listened to several phones ringing.

"Hey, Jimmy," one man said. "Carlos wants two K on Gigawatt to win at Belmont."

"No," Jimmy said. "He's into us for two grand already. Tell him to pay up first, and then we'll talk."

A toilet flushed.

"What the hell, *stunad*, who said you could leave the front?"

"I had to go."

Callum had probable cause. He glanced over his shoulder and hand-signaled to move forward, and Matheson nodded. He drew his service revolver with a swift movement as Callum kicked open the door.

"NYPD. Everybody on the floor with your hands on your

head. Play it cool, and most of you can go home. Jimmy Mack, stay standing and put your hands behind your head."

Jimmy Mack, the one man that remained standing, glared at him and held out his hands as if ready to get cuffed.

"Let my guys go. They aren't the ones you want."

## 6

## HEATHER

"I appreciate you helping me tonight," Master William said. "Carlo deserves a night off, and Samantha is staying with Lexi, while Cash is out of town for a business deal."

Heather leaned against the doorjamb of Master William's office with her arms folded. William sat in his chair behind his white desk. Everything in the room was white—the desk, the wood chair before it, and the bookcases lining the white walls behind the desk. The only thing of a different color was the black carpet, which was the same as the carpet in the atrium. It was a measure of William's meticulousness that there wasn't a smudge or speck of dust anywhere in the room.

"Not a problem, Master William. I have extra time on my hands lately."

An inscrutable expression crossed his face. "Miss Kristal *is* a newlywed."

Heather grimaced. *More than that.* But Heather had promised to keep Kristal's secret, so she wouldn't tell Master William Kristal's joyful news. "You'll be an aunty!" Kristal had squealed. Heather did her best to plaster a smile on her face and tried not to think of how this child would drive a wedge between her and her best friend. It was an unworthy thought, and Heather stuffed it down deep inside her, where she stuck things she did not want to contemplate.

"You do look spectacular. Where did you get that magenta leather?"

"It's a custom dye job. I send them a color swatch, and they send it back within two months. It's where I got all the white leather for Heather's wedding outfit."

"You are masterful with lea—"

The front door creaked open, and William glanced at his watch.

"It's early. I didn't think to lock the door, and I didn't expect—"

"Hello?" A deep voice came from the atrium.

Heather groaned. "It's Big Red."

"Pardon?"

"Everyone's favorite NYC detective."

"Oh, Callum Reilly. Yes, I invited him. Did I forget to tell him the time?" William rose from behind his desk and disappeared into the darkened atrium of the club. Heather sucked on her lip, wondering if she should follow. She huffed and moved to the Juice Bar, one room from the club's entrance, and checked the stock levels of the coolers. Two glass-fronted coolers stood at the wall, and two juice machines rested on a table next to them. On her right was a counter with a rarely used wet bar behind it. Heather moved behind the counter and checked the ice maker under the lip of the counter. Yep, filled with ice. In an hour, she'd fill the ice buckets beside the juice machines. She also pulled out the popcorn for the popcorn machine that stood against the wall to her left. William used the machine's aroma to mask the scent of physical exertion that came with BDSM play. She measured out the popcorn and added it and the oil to the popper and switched on the machine.

"Oh, there you are, Miss Heather," William said. "I need to call my wife. Will you show Mr. Reilly the club before our other guests arrive?"

With her back still turned to Master William, Heather resisted the urge to huff out a breath of frustration. After this morning's weird encounter with him, she decided it would be best to keep him at a professional distance. The last thing she needed during this tumultuous time was to get involved with a New York City cop. She told herself it had nothing to do with avoiding a relationship. This was another *bon mot* that Kristal slung at her when her best friend pressed for more details about Heather's encounter with Big Red.

"Sure, Master William, I'm happy to help." Her words threatened to stick in her throat, but she forced them out.

William smiled at her and then turned away to leave her alone with Big Red.

The popcorn popped and spilled out of the cooking cup. The aroma and the sound filled the small room.

"That's a real popcorn machine? Not a decoration? Isn't that weird for a bondage club?"

"It has a purpose."

Callum leaned against the doorjamb.

"Such as?"

Heather grabbed a large paper cup and scooped it full with the freshly popped treat. She held out to the detective, who took it. "The aroma of popcorn hides the scent of club members, um, enjoying their activities."

She couldn't resist using her professionally groomed seduction voice, and the detective coughed up a piece of popcorn.

Heather crossed to the cooler and pulled out a bottle of water and handed it to him.

"Easy there, Detective. You wouldn't want the paramedic hauling you out of a BDSM club. Might not be good for your image."

Callum drank the water in long gulps and then tossed the bottle into the recycling bin by the door.

He scoffed. "You are something."

"You have *no* idea. So, take a look. If you are *curious* about anything, just ask."

When Heather passed the detective, she glanced over her shoulder and tilted her head to gaze into his eyes. He narrowed his, and she tossed him a knowing smile. This tactic usually unnerved subs, who dread people discovering their submissive desires.

*Why are you treating him like a sub?* Heather bit her lip reflexively as this question crossed her mind, and his eyes widened.

"I do have a question. Do you tease every man you meet, or am I a special recipient of your charms?"

Heather smiled. *Is it wrong to enjoy getting under his skin?* she thought. *No. Men love it, at least the men that I like. If he doesn't enjoy it, it's just another sign he's not for me.*

She smoothed the hair over her ear with her hand and smiled seductively at him. "Trust me, Detective, you aren't that special."

The detective gave her a smoldering stare, and her breathing hitched, and parts of her tingled that had no business doing so.

*Liar, liar, pants on fire. You're so hot for him, you sizzle, and your panties have taken up smoking.* And then a sudden realization chilled her. Heather acted like a sub testing a Dom's limits. It was part of the subtle dance of sub and Dom beginning a relationship.

*Oh, hell, no.*

"You know what they say about people who say, 'Trust me,'" he said.

"No?"

"You can't trust them."

Heather creased her eyebrow because her next thought aroused her more.

*I should spank you.*

It was luscious to think of him under her riding crop. She needed to stop thinking like that now.

"Show me around the club."

He didn't even phrase it as a question. Heather regarded him again. Did she have a "baby" Dom before her?

*It might be fun to train him.*

*You are so naughty, Miss Heather Skye. What did you decide? To keep a professional arm's length between you?*

She walked down the hall and swore the detective's eyes burned into her swaying derriere.

"Now, here on the right is the costume room. You can choose a costume to rent for the evening or to buy if you so like."

"Hmm, is that William's office?" He pointed to the shut door on the left.

"Yes."

"When might he have time to speak to me?"

"I don't keep his schedule."

"But you work here, right? Why wouldn't you know?"

Heather shook her head. "No. I don't work here. I'm lending a hand for the evening since his usual help is taking the night off, and Master William's wife is doing something else. It's the least I can do for all he's done for Kristal and me."

"Such as?"

"He lent us part of the money to open Shop: BIO, and he buys a significant amount of our leather goods for resale here at the club."

The detective's attention snapped into focus. His eyes bore

into hers as if demanding answers to a burning question. But she couldn't imagine what that question would be.

"Does that include riding crops?"

"No. I don't make crops. But come with me, and I'll show you something." Heather strode ahead into the sizeable redbrick-walled room of what used to be a sweatshop. William had refinished the floor to a high gloss and painted the large window black to block out curious eyes. Unique pieces of art hung in the window wells displaying different BDSM scenes. Heather heard Callum stop walking, and she turned to find him staring at the pictures.

"Is there something there that captures your interest?"

Callum turned his gaze from one picture. That of a woman bent forward, clutching the back of a wood office chair. The woman was dressed in high spiked heels, a black corset, and a G-string, with her butt jutted to display its rounded glory. The picture was black-and-white with her lips painted a cherry red and read stipes burned across her rear. She looked over her shoulder with an adoring gaze to someone out of the frame of the shot.

Callum raked his eyes the length of her body, seeming to drink in every curve. Involuntarily, he licked his lips.

"Show me where you keep the crops."

"Of course," she said too huskily. Her face flushed with heat, and her fingers tingled. An electric current filled the space between, urging her to move closer to him as if he were a magnet. But she shook her head to snap her out of this sexual spell.

"This way," she said. Heather walked away from him quickly and entered the hallway that contained the different rooms. The first room on the right had a "2" formed in red rope. Club members used this space for personal Shibari sessions. On the left, a short riding crop stood in the place of the number one.

Master William devoted this chamber to flogging. Heather pulled the set of keys for the rooms given to her earlier by Master William and opened the door. She flicked on the light switch, revealing the room's secrets.

Floggers, whips, crops, and canes of different sizes lined either side. Spotlights lanced the lavender walls with beams of light in a march down the narrow room. A black, plush carpet covered the floor. In the middle, a bench pointed toward the back way. At the furthest end was a black Saint Andrew's Cross complete with leather cuffs to hold the submissive.

She watched Callum take in the details of the room with a cop's impassive gaze.

"I understand you were a professional Domme."

Heather's head snapped up. "Who told you that?"

He looked away and examined a flogger on the wall.

"Master William. We gossiped about you during the card game."

Heather almost chuckled. The detective had attempted to rattle her. She leaned forward and clutched the flogger he had stared at.

"I see. And what else did they say about me?"

"Not so much you, as me," Callum said. "They said I wasn't your type because you like submissive men."

He stepped forward, trying to make her step back—a Dom's move.

Heather wouldn't fall for it. She stood her ground and leveled her gaze to peer right into his eyes. She slapped the flogger in her hand.

"Is that what you need, Heather Skye? A submissive man? One who bends at your feet and kiss your toes, and says, 'Yes, Mistress. Please, another, Mistress,' as you whip him."

Heather glared at the detective.

"I am who I am, Callum Reilly. I accepted that a long time ago."

"So, there is no room in your life for this?" Callum stepped forward and wrapped his arms around her, pressing his hard length against her, as his sexy scent surrounded them. He slanted his head and captured her mouth and pressed his lips onto hers with a passion that begged Heather to submit.

# 7

## CALLUM

Callum pressed his mouth onto Heather's plump lips, and electricity sang through his body. The touch of Heather's sweet flesh against his ran through him with fire. Her kiss's addictive sweetness drove him to get closer and taste every part of her luscious body.

Her exotic floral perfume and her musk drove away rational thought. Callum's head fogged with desire. Urgency drove him to pull her hips against his shaft as it throbbed under his clothes. He sought the lace at the back of Heather's corset and tugged on it hoping to loosen the leather that held her breasts.

A sharp sting on his ass broke the spell. Surprised, Callum stepped back, not understanding where the pain came from.

Heather pulled back and held her flogger between them. Callum narrowed his eyes to see the instrument she'd used on his butt.

"What—" Callum said.

A wicked, sexy-as-sin gleam lit Heather's eyes.

Callum struggled to control his ragged breathing, while Heather didn't seem affected by their steamy kiss.

"Submissive men wouldn't ask that question—they'd ask for more."

"I'm not that type of man."

Heather sighed and turned away and sauntered to the other side of the room. The globes of her leather-clad butt rose and fell in rhythm until she reached the far wall. Pivoting, she faced Callum and reached over her head to hook a bullwhip with her fingers. Then she gave him a focused stare, smoldering with raw, dangerous sex.

*She's playing you, Reilly.*

A bit of anger rolled around in his stomach, adding to the sense of danger enveloping him.

*This woman is way above your pay grade.*

He folded his arms across his chest. "How many years did you work as a dominatrix?"

She turned and put the flogger on one of the many pegs marching down the wall. She lifted the bullwhip from the wall and turned toward him.

"Five and a half years."

"But you didn't continue the work."

"I grew tired of unreliable subs." Heather moved the leather thong through her hand while keeping a steady gaze on him. "Kristal wanted to start intimate supply parties to host in people's homes, which evolved into our business."

"I thought Master William funded your business?"

Heather cocked her head and studied him.

"Not then. We had just joined *La Corda Rosa* as members, and we ran our business out of our apartment. Then we opened a shop in Chinatown, but someone else bought the building and didn't want a 'sex' shop there. Master William planned to open a new restaurant where BIO is now, and we loved the location even if the building needs a good remodel. But why are we talking business, Detective? One would think you had ulterior motives for this little chat."

Callum's face flushed.

*There goes your professional demeanor.*

Why did this woman upend him with every word and small movement of her body?

*Because you've never met a hotter woman.*

Heather let the thong of the whip drop to the floor. She held the whip as if warding off an assault and fixed her steely gaze on him.

"Are you afraid?" Callum said.

"Why would you say that, Detective?"

"You are holding the most dangerous weapon in the room."

"Oh, I'm not, Detective. When you kissed me, I felt your weapon."

He smiled. "What I pressed against your hip is not a weapon."

She scoffed. "Your service revolver isn't a weapon?"

Callum wiped the grin from his face. "Oh, that."

"What did you think I meant?"

He looked away. Heather just kept pushing his buttons.

"Never mind. So what do the men you date enjoy?"

"Date?" she said seductively. "Or are you more curious about my work as a Domme? Is that what this little meeting is about?"

"Master William asked you to show me the club."

"Yes. But you kissed me. That was not in the party plan."

Callum rubbed the back of his head.

"Why don't you show me then what the men you date like to do?"

"Show you?"

"Or tell me. Whatever makes you comfortable."

Heather put the whip back on the wall, took a riding crop, walked to the bench, sat and crossed her legs. In doing so, she lifted one stiletto-heeled boot up while slapping her palm with the crop's shaft.

"They would kneel and kiss my feet, and beg for the privilege."

"Your subs enjoyed that?"

"They literally dreamed about kneeling at my feet. They would have long conversations over the phone about how much they shivered in delight over those thoughts."

"But why? I don't understand."

Heather's eyes glittered. "It is an intimate thing for a man to admit a need to serve a woman. It's not something we value in our culture. Society sees men as takers, women as givers, and we shame people who act otherwise. Men experience great shame and pain for not being 'man' enough. It's comforting, at least for a while, to have someone see and accept and not judge your desires."

"What about you?" Callum didn't intend the stern edge in his voice. But he didn't like the idea of Heather with other men.

*Are you nuts, Reilly? You barely know this woman.*

*I've found her attractive since we first met. That was over a year ago. It's time to do something about it.*

"What do you mean?"

Callum raised his eyebrows. "Do you dream about kissing a man's feet?"

Heather scoffed. "No. Why would I?"

"So, you've never knelt before a man."

She rolled her eyes. "I didn't say that. When I first trained as a sub, yes. You must learn what the other person experiences before you can Domme."

"So, you have kissed a man's feet?"

Heather stood suddenly and huffed.

"If I did, it was to understand the sub mindset."

"But you can't know. You don't have the same emotional reactions as a submissive person. Is that what I heard you say?"

Heather cocked her head. "Is that a detective thing you have going on? Ask probing questions to upset your prey?"

"You're not prey."

"Oh, no? Because your weapon engaged in a seek and capture mission."

"My service revolver?" Callum said.

Heather wrinkled her nose. "If you want to call it that."

"You've held a weapon in your hands since I walked in here."

Heather stood and chuckled. "It's fun to watch you try to psychoanalyze me." She touched the tip of her quirt to Callum's jawline. "Hmm. Five o'clock shadow." She ran the crop along his jaw, then turned the flat of the keeper under his chin. He could not figure out why the crop sent electric tingles through him. She gave him a good long gaze, as if analyzing him, and that made him shiver.

"What are you doing?"

"Come now, Detective, you should be used to evaluations. You are part of the police force, aren't you? Surely you get performance reviews?"

"I have done nothing yet to review."

She leaned forward, emphasizing the swell of her breasts in her corset, and then let the crop drop. With a shock, Callum realized she trailed the quirt up his inner thigh. Then she held it under his balls. She pushed the instrument upward so that he felt its pressure.

The woman was toying with him, and Callum didn't like it. Well, some of what she did he enjoyed, but the sense that she mocked him annoyed the hell out of him.

"You'd better stop that."

Heather laughed. "Or what?"

Callum didn't know what. What the hell would he do with

this gorgeous, hot, infuriating woman? His cock said yes, but his rational mind grasped her trouble potential. He didn't need that in his life. And he wanted her to stop touching him with that damned crop because he was ready to rip it out of her hand.

Finally he said, "I'll turn you over on my knee and spank you."

Heather stared him in the eye once more with a steely intensity that ran a shiver through him.

"Oooh, baby Dom." Her voice tumbled silky and too damned sexy from her mouth, and he fought the urge to rip the crop from her hand.

"What?"

"A Dominant-in-the-making. You have potential, Detective."

"Now see here—"

Heather shook her head. "No, you are the one that doesn't see. Because I'm a Domme, and you have the potential to be a Dom, we're not suited for each other."

"I think I should be the judge of what's suitable."

She shook her head. "Master William started this club for those who like to indulge in power exchange. A handsome man like you could attract a sub who'd do anything for you. But you must learn how to treat her. And you need schooling on using different accouterments in BDSM play."

"What are you suggesting?"

"I think Master William would be up for you joining the club with my recommendation. And he enjoys mentoring new Doms."

"You're offering to sponsor my membership?"

"If I need to, but again, on my recommendation, another member here would sponsor you."

"Are you trying to sell me a membership?" Callum couldn't keep an incredulous tone from his voice.

"You discuss money with Master William. I have no stake in this at all, except to help strengthen club membership."

Callum couldn't believe this. One minute, he kissed the hottest woman he ever met, and the next, she offered him a membership in an exclusive BDSM club.

*Don't quibble, Reilly. You got yourself in. Take it.*

"Okay. But I have one condition."

"What's that?"

"That *you* give me Dom lessons."

# 8

## HEATHER

W̲HOA THERE, COWBOY.

Heather stepped back from the sexy detective and shook her head.

"Several member Doms enjoy tutoring new Doms. Master Cash is an excellent choice, though he won't be here tonight.

Callum narrowed his eyes.

"No."

Heather shrugged. "Suit yourself, but you don't want me as a teacher."

"Why not?" Callum shot Heather a fiery gaze.

Nope. Nada. Not happening. She did not need this complication. Teaching a baby Dom that devoured her body with his eyes? Not a good idea. A nice submissive girl would make Callum happy, not a wild child like Heather, who couldn't behave to save her life. It didn't matter that she burned for the sexy detective, too. The incendiary passion negated a teacher-student dynamic.

"You might not enjoy my tutelage. I am a strict Mistress."

"I'm a s—I mean, cop. I can handle it."

Heather pursed her lips, wondering what that slip of the

tongue meant. She studied his determined expression. Yes, he could endure Heather's course of study, but as a Dom personality, he wouldn't like it.

*He's just using this as an excuse to get close to me, and I will not let that happen.*

"Then let me demonstrate. You might not like it."

"Do your worst."

Heather paced the room's length to a group of floggers in different sizes and finishes at the ends. Each had a different weight and feel. She selected the lightest one and crooked her finger to direct him to step closer.

With a face steeled against emotion, Callum complied. Heather jutted her chin and straightened her back. Even with her spiked heels, Callum stood four inches above her.

"Stretch out your hand," she commanded.

"Will you slap my hand again? I remember the crop in your store."

"Don't ask questions. Do as I say."

"Okay."

She dropped her voice an octave to underscore her next words. "The correct answer is 'Yes, Mistress Heather.'"

He lowered his head and looked at her with disbelief.

"Really?"

"If you want a sub to show you the proper respect, learn to give it. A sub is a precious gift, and despite what people think, you do not abuse them. Part of that is showing them respect. That is also very important at *La Corda Rosa*. You notice that we use titles here such as Master William, Miss, or Mistress Heather, Mr. Reilly."

"Yes. I noticed. I thought it was an affectation."

She shook her head. "No. It may sound old-fashioned, but it's how we respect our members. Master William sets the standard. So, show me respect, or this mini-lesson is over."

"What? You won't spank me?" His eyes glittered wickedly.

"Mr. Reilly. What you are doing is what we call 'topping from the bottom.' A good Dom or Domme will not tolerate it. This is your last warning. Hold out your hand."

His mouth formed a grim line. "Yes, Mistress Heather."

"Good," she said with a nod. "Now show your palms."

Callum held them out, and she struck both with the light flogger.

He scrunched up his eyebrows again. "I barely felt the leather."

"This one is more symbolic than painful. It's lightweight, and if you worked it too hard, not only would you tire your wrist, it would fall apart." She hung that one up and selected a more massive flogger with knotted tresses. "This one, if you struck too hard, would flay flesh. We must use care with this flogger. Let me demonstrate." Heather held out her arm and gave it a hard strike with the instrument. Small beads of blood welled where the knots hit.

"You didn't have to go that far," protested Callum. He stepped forward and pulled her arm to him. She tried to pull it away, but he held it fast and stared into her eyes.

She swallowed hard. He stood too close, and she caught his sexy scent. Her knees wobbled, her heart danced the Conga, and she couldn't find her breath. Had she ever wanted a man this much? Her eyes lit on the bench in the center of the room, and in her mind's eye, she saw herself and Callum in an intimate embrace.

God, she wanted that man in the worst way, which was terrible.

She closed her eyes.

"Don't," she said. *Don't want me. We'd never make each other happy.* She couldn't force out those words, so she hoped that one word was sufficient.

"I don't think I can stop," he said in a husky voice.

"Understand—"

"What?" Callum demanded.

She shook her head violently and tears misted at the corners of her eyes.

She twisted her arm and yanked it away hard. Her wrist burned. She thought it best to get a reminder of how a man could hurt her. She'd let no one get this close in such a long time she had almost forgotten. She stepped back and placed one hand on her hip.

"We're done with this lesson," Heather said sternly. "I am disappointed in your performance, Mr. Reilly. Discipline is an important part of BDSM. A Dom must learn to control his desires, so he doesn't harm his sub. BDSM play is very intense, and a sub will easily get carried away in the experience. As the person who controls the scene, it's important that you not lose your composure."

He opened his mouth as if to speak, but a knock on the door shattered the moment between them.

"Miss Heather?"

"Yes, Master William. Please enter."

William walked in and surveyed the charged atmosphere with his keen eyes. He tossed Heather a quizzical glance.

"Mr. Reilly would like to join *La Corda Rosa*. I believe he has excellent potential to become a Dom."

Master William smiled warmly. "Your instincts are always excellent, Miss Heather. And we can arrange something for you, Mr. Reilly. However, I need Heather at the front desk. Mingle. Aaron will arrive soon, and he can tell you more about the club. And Miss Heather, I forgot to ask you, but I'd appreciate it if you stand in for Miss Samantha during my Shibari presentation."

"Of course, Master William. My pleasure. Excuse me, Mr. Reilly. I need to check in our guests."

Heather strode from the two men as fast as her spiked heels could take her and reached the front desk. She spent the next hour greeting and signing in guests until the last one on the night's list checked in. The work almost kept her from thinking about a certain copper-topped detective until she sensed him in the hallway. It wasn't just his cologne she picked up. An energetic connection seemed to draw Heather to Callum and enveloped her with his warm presence. The closer he came, the more magnetic the pull.

She worried what she would say should he show up at her elbow, demanding more of her than she could give.

*You need to fight this.*

Still, she couldn't resist peeking around the corner. Oddly, she didn't see him.

*Where did he go?*

Heather wrinkled her nose. The club wasn't large, and *La Corda Rosa* didn't lose guests.

The front door opened, and Heather's attention snapped forward. An unfamiliar elderly man stepped inside. He cast his gaze around the atrium, taking it in, and then his eyes lit on Heather.

The man stood about 5' 7" with an extremely lean frame held up by his black cane. A white semi-circle of hair fringed a nearly bald head. But his eyes carried the alertness of a hawk, and he turned that gaze on Heather.

"What a lovely sight. Gil always had the best taste in women."

"Pardon me?" Heather said stiffly.

"I'm here to see Gil."

"Sorry?"

"Gil Ianucci, though I suppose you call him William."

"Master William," she said.

The man shook his head in disbelief. "Master William." He

sighed. "In any case, tell Gil his Uncle Gitchy, that's Doctor Gabriel Russo to you, is here."

Heather did not like Dr. Gabriel Russo. He didn't fit in here, and she didn't trust he had honorable motives.

"Master William is busy with guests."

"I don't care what he's doing. I wouldn't be here unless I have important business with him. Now, go get Gil."

Gitchy glowered at her, and Heather twitched her mouth and blew out a breath.

"I'll tell him, but I won't make promises."

"I'll wait in his office." Gitchy glared at her with an expression that told her that he wouldn't take no for an answer. Who was he to tell Heather what he'd do in Master William's club?

"Excuse me?" said Heather indignantly. But Gitchy ignored her and walked right past the desk and straight to Master William's office. Clearly, he had been here before this, though Heather had not met him. He pushed the door open.

"Who the hell are you?" growled Gitchy.

Heather rushed forward to investigate the fracas and found Gitchy facing off with Callum.

"Mr. Reilly?" Heather said. "What are you doing in Master William's office?"

"Yes," Gitchy said. "What are you doing here? You have the smell of 'cop' all over you."

"Dr. Russo," Heather said. "Mr. Reilly is a police detective here at Master William's invitation. We'd thank you not to treat him rudely."

"Look, little girl, I've been dealing with his type all my life. If you have a police detective in your house, you have trouble."

Heather shot Gitchy an angry glance. No one called her "little girl" and lived to tell the tale even if he was old enough to be her grandfather.

"What is going on?"

They all turned to Master William standing in the doorway.

"Uncle Gitchy, what are you doing here?" The perplexed expression on Master William's face told her that he did not expect Gitchy at his club.

"I came to talk to you. I didn't think I'd find a police detective."

"Can we talk another time? I'm—"

"Don't tell me how busy you are, Gil. There's shit hitting that you need to know about."

"Okay, Uncle Gitchy, I'm sure everything is fine. Mr. Reilly, please, give us a few minutes, and I'll be right with you. Miss Heather, please escort Mr. Reilly to the demonstration room while I speak with my uncle."

"He *is* your uncle?" Heather said. She had met all of Master William's family, and none were as rude as this man.

"More like an old family friend, so we've always called him uncle." William held out his hand, inviting both Heather and Callum to leave.

Heather walked past Master William and then looked back at Gitchy, who appeared unconcerned about the upset he'd brewed. Callum's expression turned grim as William shut the door.

"You don't know who Gitchy is, do you?" Callum said.

"No, I never met him. And how would you?"

Callum shrugged. "I'm a cop. It's my job to know the major crime figures on my beat."

Heather frowned. "Master William doesn't mess with crime," she declared.

Callum looked away.

"Come to think of it, Mr. Cop, what were you doing in Master William's office?"

# 9

## CALLUM

Callum resisted the urge to glance over his shoulder to William Ianucci's office. He wished he was a fly on the wall there because Dr. Gabriel's arrival at *La Corda Rosa* confirmed his suspicions. While not on the top rung of the New York City's crime hierarchy, Russo's connections insured the FBI had surveilled the mobster on and off for the past four decades.

"Mr. Reilly." Heather's scolding tone snagged his attention. He snapped his head toward her. Damn. How did she do that?

"Move along. The fun part lies beyond, not here in this hallway."

"You sure?" Callum said with a wink. "I'm having plenty of fun."

"Down, boy. I've told you I'm not your type of girl."

"Maybe I'm not Mr. Right. But I could be Mr. Right Now."

Heather scoffed. "Boy, you lack the octane in your fuel tank to chase me."

Damn. The Domme was tough.

Callum stepped two paces closer to her to stand barely six inches from her back. "Are you sure?"

Heather glared at him over her shoulder when her feet hit

the wood floor of *La Corda Rosa's* primary room. "That's Miss Heather to you, Mr. Reilly. The club membership gathers here. Mix with anyone but me."

Callum scanned the room filled with clients of *La Corda Rosa*. Many of them, dressed in leather, chatted as if they were attending a costume party. Many of the women wore leather corsets, stockings, and boots. He'd witnessed strippers dressed less sexily. The men either wore suits or leather pants and vests.

"Miss Heather," hailed a man from across the room. Heather swiveled her head and smiled.

"Here's a man for you to meet, Mr. Reilly."

Heather strode through the crowd without glancing back, as if she expected him to follow her. And he did. Heather's lovely round bottom swayed sexily in her thigh-high leather boots. His brain danced to the rhythmic click of Heather's stiletto heels. So what if they weren't right for each other? He couldn't promise forever. His job kept him mobile, and he didn't know where he'd be one day to the next. His current investigation had been in his most extended posting in his career, and he had four short weeks to make his case. A lasting relationship was not on his to-do list. But that didn't prevent him from having fun, and he'd like it with Heather.

Heather stopped before an older man with salt-and-pepper hair dressed casually in white button-down and khaki slacks. He peered at Callum with sharp blue eyes.

"Master Paul, let me introduce you to Mr. Reilly. He's Aaron's friend."

Master Paul extended a hand and smiled warmly. "Any friend of Aaron's is a friend of mine, too."

"Mr. Reilly has expressed a desire to join the club."

Heather spoke the word "desire" suggestively, and Callum swallowed.

"Glad to hear it."

"I suggested he take a mentor as he explores his Dom nature," Heather said perkily, as if discussing a bauble she'd picked up in a store.

"That's a wise idea. Nothing worse than starting without the proper training and having someone get hurt."

"Are you here with anyone, Master Paul?"

"Not tonight."

"Then please do me a favor and show Mr. Reilly the club until Aaron arrives. I'm helping Master William tonight."

"Anything for you, Mistress Heather."

"You're so sweet," Heather said. "If you didn't play for the other team, I'd snatch you myself."

Master Paul laughed. "You're bad, Miss Heather. As intriguing as that sounds, two dominants? I don't see it working."

"Perhaps not. Shame. Well, lovely to see you again, Master Paul, Mr. Reilly."

Heather trotted away as lightly as a spring colt, and Callum couldn't help but follow her with his eyes until she left the room.

"So, the lovely Miss Heather caught your attention?" Master Paul said.

"She is something," Callum said.

"There are many men here who think the same thing, but she is particular."

Callum grimaced. "You mean the 'she only likes submissive men' thing? Honestly, I don't understand it."

"But you like submissive women?"

"But that's different."

An amused expression spread over the Dom's face. "It is?" he said. "How's that? Because men shouldn't be submissive?"

"You could say."

Paul shook his head with a grin on his face. "I see."

Callum saw his mistake. In front of him was a gay Dom. Of course, he liked submissive men. "I mean, whatever floats your boat."

"If you don't understand the lure of submission, then how can you know if you're a dominant?"

The question knocked him back. Callum never questioned the assumptions of what made a man. And now, standing close to a person who called himself a Dom, questions entered Callum's head. He was a soldier who had been at the front lines of war. While it was okay for a man to take the lead, he couldn't imagine letting his lover do so.

"I expect to be in charge," Callum said. "Don't you?"

"Of course. I own a substantial business and have many employees who depend on me, so yes, I am in control. But that differs from a Dom/sub relationship. On the outside, it may look as if the Dom is the controlling partner. But it's more subtle than that. Submissives want to please, but they also need to *allow* someone to control the scenes. It gives them a sense of security to play by a set of clearly defined rules. But if you don't provide your sub what they need, that relationship will end. And matching the needs of Dom and sub is a tricky proposition from the start."

"Are you saying the Dom submits to the sub?"

Master Paul smiled. "In a vanilla relationship, each person keeps their power and meets in the middle. But in a Dom/sub relationship, the two partners exchange it. The sub offers their submission for experiences few can give them. It takes communication, agreements, and honesty to navigate a power exchange. And here's the secret. I don't do whatever I desire to a sub. I plan the scene around what the sub wants."

"Wait? Are you telling me you serve your submissive?"

"No. I'm saying I'm focused on what he wants, to get what I want."

"And what would that be?"

Master Paul gave a wry grin. "Pleasure."

Heather returned wearing a pensive expression. "Master Paul, Master William got hung up on personal business. He asked you to perform the Shibari demonstration tonight."

Master Paul glanced toward the direction from which Heather had walked. "Is everything okay?"

"He says yes. It's a matter that can't wait."

"And who is my model?"

"I am. If you don't mind."

"Mistress Heather, my pleasure. After you."

Callum cast his eyes toward Ianucci's office, though it was impossible to see it from that angle. But with Heather and Paul leaving him alone on the floor, he could investigate what business Russo had with William Ianucci.

"Mr. Reilly?"

Callum turned toward the voice to find Master Paul waving for him to join Heather and him under a set of spotlights. He shook his head. Callum knew nothing of BDSM or Shibari and had no business standing next to those two.

"Everyone," Master Paul said. "This is Mr. Reilly. We're considering him for club membership. He seems to be a touch shy." A sprinkling of laughter rose from the gallery at the remark.

Callum blew out a breath of frustration and moved toward the pair since he could not leave the hall without the club patrons noticing. He walked to Paul and Heather, aware of the eyes on him. And he wondered why Master Paul had called him.

But as he stepped into the spotlight, the gallery spectators applauded. Callum blinked because he did not expect this reaction.

Master Paul reached for a bag by the wall and drew out two

lengths of coiled red rope. He handed one to Callum, who stared at it.

"Miss Heather, please dress for the demonstration while I show Mr. Reilly the rudiments of handling rope."

"I'll be right back." Heather hurried from the two men and disappeared into the crowd.

"I like what she's wearing," Callum said as his eyes followed her.

The patrons laughed.

"Don't we all? But for Shibari, we want our models to have as few restrictions on their bodies as possible to ensure we tie knots correctly with a minimum of stress on their bodies. Shibari, done right, is art. It is torture if done wrong."

"I'm confused," Callum said. "This is a BDSM club?"

"The 'B' in that acronym stands for bondage. And Shibari is the ultimate form of that. But before you can start, you must learn to handle the rope."

Callum winced and pushed a horrible memory away. He didn't want to concentrate on that day now.

"First," Paul continued, "choose your rope for the play you'll engage in. You can find them in different materials such as cotton, silk, bamboo, nylon, jute, and hemp. Each has different tensile strengths and degrees of softness. For light bondage in the bedroom, cotton and silk are excellent choices, though silk is much more expensive than cotton. They give you the control you need without placing undue stress on your play partner's skin. Bamboo has antibacterial properties. You use that for, um, sensitive areas. But tonight, we will do suspension work, and that requires a strong and supple rope. What you hold in your hand is hemp. It's strong, with a good grip that doesn't allow slippage in the knots."

"And that's important?"

"The whole of the tie depends on the strength of the other ties. If one knot slips, then you can harm your model."

"Show him how to do it!" called a spectator. A murmur of agreement ran through the crowd.

"I will," Master Paul said with a smile. With a quick flick of his wrist, the rope uncoiled, and one end fell to the floor. "There are ropes of different footage, but we'll start with twenty-foot lengths. Go ahead. Uncoil your line."

Callum sought the end of the rope to pull it free, and he did, but with more concentration than Master Paul.

"Now, just for today, pull the length against your palm, and grab the other end."

Callum did as Master Paul instructed, and to his surprise, the rope fibers were soft instead of scratchy as he expected.

"It's soft," he said.

"Yes. We treat it with hemp oil to condition the rope. Now, fold over one end." Master Paul bent the rope to form one. "We call this loop the byte. Ah, here is Miss Heather now."

Callum looked up from his rope, and his mouth dropped open. Heather trotted to the spotlighted area, dressed in a lowcut, tight-fitting sleeveless one-piece bodysuit. It left nothing to the imagination, especially her rear, where the suit looked like a thong. He swallowed hard. He didn't think Heather could be any sexier, but this outfit made him want to lose it on the stage.

"Lovely," Master Paul said.

"We carry these tank thongs in our shop."

"They are perfect for what we will do. Are you ready, Mr. Reilly?"

Callum couldn't pull his gaze from Heather in the tank thong. The garment revealed every luscious curve and highlighted the round globes of her perfect ass.

"Sure," he said.

# 10

## HEATHER

The heated stare Callum gave Heather prickled goosebumps on her skin. She liked how the tank thong covered parts north and south in one stretchy piece of fabric that clung scandalously to her body. But she hated how Callum raked her body with his eyes. Callum's idea they should date was monumentally disastrous because he did not understand her.

Heather could switch from Domme to sub when she wanted, as many BDSM practitioners did. But the sub role didn't give her as much satisfaction as the Domme role, and a vanilla lifestyle bored her agile mind. Callum and she were worlds apart in relationship needs, and she didn't understand why Master Paul asked Callum to take part in this demonstration.

She rubbed her bare thighs with her hands as butterflies fluttered in her stomach. Master Paul continued showing Callum how to handle the rope. Callum's proximity shot dangerous tingles through her body, and she eyed the room's exits for likely escape routes. But she had promised Master William that she would help because Shibari demonstrations were popular with club members.

Master Paul directed his words to Callum but spoke loud

enough for the patrons to hear. "Shibari is a dangerous activity. It is important as the rigger to pay the ultimate attention to your model. Tie the rope tighter than you should, you restrict blood flow. Too loose and the tie holds your model securely, and she or he falls into the rope, and blood flow gets restricted. Your model can fall into subspace during the experience, so he or she will not notice until it is too late if there is a problem with the ropes. Miss Heather, I'm ready to begin."

"Yes, Master Paul."

The Dom winked at her before stepping to her back. Without warning, he lowered a strip of silk over her eyes. She blinked, and her eyelashes fluttered against the lustrous fabric.

She did not expect the blindfold. The lack of sight made her concentrate on her remaining senses. Right now, Master Paul wore Tom Ford's Tuscan Leather, a luxurious fragrance. But Heather found the raspberry top note too sweet despite the leather and wood undertones. Callum's scent was much more intriguing, full of delicious musk and sandalwood, and this was an unwelcome distraction.

"You can either wrap the rope twice or knot the byte and leave and draw the cord around. I prefer doubling the rope, so I have the byte available in the back."

Master Paul took her shoulder and turned her away from the audience. He lifted her arms, then wrapped the double rope around under her arms. The tug of the first knot he made was a gentle affirmation of his intent and settled Heather into the sub mindset. She needed to do nothing but to allow him to work. He turned her to face front.

He stuck two fingers between the rope. "Two fingers correctly gauge if the rope is too tight or loose," he said.

"I see," rumbled Callum. Damn it. The timbre of his voice, laden with lust, sent shivers through her.

*Stop it. Stop being so sexy.*

Confusion swamped her brain. She liked submissive men, and Callum was not one. Why should he check off her "sexy as hell" box? It shouldn't happen.

"Here," Master Paul said. "Try for yourself."

Heather felt the heat emanating from Callum's body as he drew closer to her. She closed her eyes as he stuck two fingers between the rope and the skin above her breast. The slow and steady slide sent a jolt through her. She refused to voice a small whine coming from deep within her, and it stuck in her throat.

"Shh," whispered Master Paul in her ear. "Relax."

He laid his hand on the back of Heather's neck to reassure her, as any Dom would reassure a skittish bottom.

*Did he think I do not know what to expect?* Heather lifted her head and kept her blindfolded eyes forward, resolved to get through this demonstration like the former professional she was. She should enjoy this rare opportunity, not dreading it because of the detective that stood next to her.

Paul began the upper wrap. Because this wrap would be a suspension, he would need to craft a secure torso harness. He continued his ties, turning her as he needed to show the audience the ties. She knew this weave because she had done it with one particular client who enjoyed roped binding their body. It took weeks for her to master. A man's body was not the same and didn't have the same architecture in the front to anchor the rope. Master Paul must have been thinking the same thing in reverse. Still, he worked steady, drawing the length through and under, looping and knotting the rope to make the weave secure. He was meticulous and checked the tension of his work regularly, and the more he worked, the less Heather could move. She relaxed into the weave.

"How are you doing, Miss Heather?" Master Paul said.

His voice sounded far away. She wasn't flying. Not yet. But

she was in the place where the day-to-day receded into a pleasurable haze.

"Fine," she said faintly.

"Anything too tight? Anything tingling?"

"Is she okay?" Callum asked with concern.

"Check the ropes."

To object meant pulling herself out of that drowsy place, and she didn't want that. Heather enjoyed Callum's calloused fingers running along her flesh. The goosebumps returned, accompanied by a warm sensation in her stomach and between her legs. This was the delicious part of submission, where desire kicks in, but you have released control and cannot act on your impulses.

How did Callum's hands get so rough? New York City men, at least the ones she knew, were well-groomed, like Master Paul. His hands were as smooth as her own. But Callum's had the feel of a man engaged in rough work. Just what was his story? Even a New York City detective wouldn't have the hands of a dock worker.

Immersed in her speculations, she didn't notice that Master Paul had finished the pelvic girdle.

"You okay?" Callum asked.

"Um-hum," murmured Heather.

"I will attach the suspension ropes to the back of Miss Heather's harness to give her stability while I work on the rest of the pose," Master Paul said.

The ring above her head jangled, and Master Paul tossed rope through it and pulled. The vibration of Master Paul's sliding another cord through the weave on her back thrummed through the ropes. The taut line lifted her feet from the floor. But as Master Paul said, this gave her body support as he lifted her leg.

"Hold this," Master Paul said, and Callum's rough hand

supported the leg that Master Paul bent. Paul wove and knotted a rope at her pelvic girdle and swiftly lashed her leg in place.

"Put your hands in front of you, please, Miss Heather."

Many riggers tied the hands first, and with good reason. But the hands were the first to tire. Heather appreciated that he didn't. But with the coming suspension, he must bind her hands. He spun her on the rope line to the ceiling, and the world tilted sending Heather into to that delicious place of white haze that felt so good.

"You can release the leg now," Master Paul said to Callum.

The detective drew his hand away with reluctance as if he didn't want to stop touching her.

*But you must, Mr. Reilly. I am not for you.*

Or she could have imagined his reluctance. But she did not imagine that his scent grew stronger. Heather took in the scent of his sweat, which was a male involuntary response to arousal. She imagined his hard cock inside his jeans and him not being able to do anything about it. It was a delicious thought. The Domme in her enjoyed making a man sweat.

With her wrists touching pulse point to pulse point, Master Paul lashed her wrists together and using the line, pulled her hand over her head. She could flex the one foot she had on the ground to make herself hang just like that.

A hand caressed the line of her jaw. If Master Paul was a lover, at this point in the show, he might kiss her. And a light kiss graced her cheek. But with a shock, she realized it was Callum that did so.

"I hope you don't mind," whispered Callum. "He told me to do it."

*Likely story.*

But she found she didn't mind. The gentle, caring kiss spread an encompassing warmth through Heather she'd never experienced before. She relished the sensation, and that was a problem.

With more tugging on the line, Master Paul wove straight and bent leg together with rope. With a pull, her one foot lifted from the ground, and her heart caught in her throat as her head fell backward. Unable to move, she felt the rope cradle and caress her, and she was as secure as a child held in her mother's arms. Master Paul, Callum Reilly, and the club all seemed far away as she climbed the high that subspace gave her. The drop halted, suspending her horizontally in the air.

Master Paul was at her side, and with another yank of the rope, she twisted to the side, but it didn't matter. She existed in another place, not on this earth. Vaguely she discerned applause from the gallery, but it had nothing to do with her.

She was flying.

Relaxed and at peace, all her cares fell away. She needn't worry about her best friend moving on with her life, or the leatherwork that sat on her leather bench, or moving in with a friend of a friend, a girl she barely knew, or even if Callum Reilly wanted more than she could give him. It had been a long time since she enjoyed the high that subspace could bring, and she intended to savor every bit.

Not that she formed these thoughts cogently. They were half-formed and mixed in the swirl of pleasure that engulfed her mind. It was better than getting drunk because she didn't need to navigate a room full of people to get out of a club or bar or fend off handsy men who didn't understand she had zero interest in them. She trusted Master Paul to care for her, and that was pure gold.

But then a rude noise shocked her to wakefulness.

"The fire alarm," Callum said. "Is there a fire exit?"

"Yes," Master Paul said.

"Get these people out that door."

"But Miss Heather—"

"I'll get her. Get these people out."

"Everyone, go to the back door. Follow me. This is the way out."

Heather heard a click, and she fell, but into muscular arms.

"Hold on," Callum said. "I'll rescue you."

## 11

Heather shivered under Callum's arm even though it was a warm New York City night as he walked her to the street from the club's back exit. In the distance, a police siren split the night in typical city fashion. Three police cars and two fire trucks sat on the street at the back and side of the block with their emergency lights strobing while chatter from their radios spilled into the night. Club patrons gathered in clumps and Callum scanned the group for the club owner or his infamous uncle but did not spot them.

Heather shivered again.

"You okay?" he asked.

Heather's teeth chattered as she nodded her head.

"You don't look okay."

Master Paul approached and unfolded a mylar blanket.

"Let me put this on you, Heather," he said. She nodded, and he draped the blanket over her shoulders.

"I'll be okay," she said.

"Of course, Mistress Heather," assured Paul.

"Is she okay? Should an EMT check her out?"

"No," Paul said. "She's experiencing subdrop, when the feel-good chemicals in her body from our session dissolve."

"Like when someone suffers shock?" Callum had seen combat buddies in shock after a rough battle, and he swallowed hard at the idea that what they did in the club would cause Heather harm.

"Something like that. Not quite. But she'll be okay. Heather just needs someone to watch her for a while."

Callum frowned. He couldn't be that person. Right now he had to attend to what happened in the club and find out where Ianucci and Russo had disappeared.

"Can you stay with her? I need to check on something," Callum said.

"Of course," Master Paul said. "But do return."

"Sure," Callum said. "Heather, I'll be back as soon as I'm done."

Heather shivered again, and Callum walked grimly to the uniformed officer he saw.

"Detective Reilly," Callum said. He held up his badge. "Who has charge of the scene?"

"Sergeant Emmons," the officer said. "He's around the corner."

"Thanks."

Callum walked around the block and found an officer wearing sergeant's stripes staring down the alley toward the club entrance.

"Sergeant Emmons, I'm Detective Reilly."

Emmons shot him a cursory glance. "What can I do for you, Detective?"

"Was there a fire?"

Emmons scowled. "No. As far as I can tell, someone pulled the alarm as a prank. Don't these people have anything better to do?"

"I don't think it was a prank, Sergeant, but a cover for certain people to get away in the commotion."

"Oh?"

"Have you seen the owner of the club? William Ianucci?"

"Ianucci? From the family that owns Romallo's Restaurant?"

"The same."

Emmons shrugged. "No. Haven't seen any Ianuccis. He owns this club? What goes on in there? Some things look downright freaky."

"Oh, come on, Sergeant. Don't tell me you've never seen a BDSM club?"

"My wife would freaking kill me. You've been in there?"

Callum frowned. "I'm working on a case."

"And is Ianucci involved in your case?"

"That's what I'm trying to find out."

"Well, I'd like to speak with Ianucci, to find out if anything went missing so I can log it in my report. Or if he knew who pulled that alarm."

"Has the fire department cleared the building? I'd like to look. And there are a couple people here who can tell me if anything is missing."

Emmons drew his eyebrows together. "Who are they?"

"Club members. I have an in with them."

The sergeant twisted his mouth. "You can go in. The firefighters report no fire damage. They are checking the other two other floors—"

Two other floors? Of course he had seen the windows for the other floors, but seeing that the club was only on the first floor, he didn't think about those. He just assumed other people rented them. And that got him thinking about New York's subway system, which harbored old unused platforms and tunnels. Did Iannucci's building have a secret entrance to this subterranean world he could use for an escape? He must ask Heather if she knew anything about it.

"Thank you, Sergeant. I'll update you on what I find out." He handed the sergeant his card. "So you can reach me if you need to."

"Fine, thanks." The sergeant whistled and waved to an officer standing at the door.

"This one is going in."

Callum nodded and headed to the front door, but instead of entering walked down the side alley that brought him to Heather and Master Paul.

"There's no fire, but no one has seen Ianucci. Heather, can you walk through with me and check to see if anything is missing?"

Heather bit her lip. "Master Paul, please give me a hand. Tell everyone to go home. They'll get a text when the club is open again. If they have belongings inside, text me and I'll bring them to the front door."

"That sounds like a plan."

Callum put his arm around Heather and walked her inside. "Are you okay?"

"Yes. Fine," she said curtly as she shook off his arm.

"You seemed pretty shook up."

"I'm not now, and that's just part of the experience. Just like anything in life. It feels good for a while and then you come down off the high."

Heather opened the first door on the left. "That looks okay." She moved the door on the right, but as she put her hand on the doorknob, Callum placed his hand over hers.

"Why would you do that to yourself?"

Heather sighed. "BDSM has been part of my life for a long time, and I'm not 'doing anything' to myself. I rarely take the model role in Shibari. Actually, Shibari is Master William's thing. I like good old-fashioned Domme/sub play."

She gave Callum's hand an acid glance, and he pulled it away.

"Are you telling me you couldn't have a normal relationship?"

Heather poked her head in the door of that room and then shook her head.

"No, I can't."

"But why?"

Heather's eyes narrowed. "Because a man kneeling at your feet can't kick you in the teeth. Callum, aren't you supposed to be on the job here?"

He blinked. Callum had come to *La Corda Rosa* undercover as a club guest. If he admitted he was here to investigate, he could blow things with her. From what little he knew of her, Heather would not appreciate Callum's investigating her friend.

*Right now, she doesn't appear to appreciate much about him.*

When he didn't answer, Heather rolled her eyes. "What is normal? I think men kneeling at my feet and kissing my boots is normal. Do you?"

She shot him a cutting look.

"No, of course not."

She shrugged. "Then why do you ask?"

Heather opened the next door on the right and poked her head in.

"So far I see nothing out of the ordinary," she said.

"I didn't see William out there. Where would he go?"

"How would I know, Reilly? It's not my day to watch him."

"And the guy he was with disappeared, too."

She shrugged. "Master William's business is his own."

*Except he may launder money for terrorist organizations. Then that's my business, at least until I must report to my commanding officer.*

The clock was not Callum's friend. A year here did nothing to help him crack this case, and he was only just getting in with the target of his investigation. If he didn't make a break in the case soon, he'd have to leave the job unfinished and he hated that thought.

Heather finished looking into the different rooms at the back of the club and walked into the large hall. Her heels clicked on the hardwood floors as she headed toward the dressing rooms. Callum walked behind her, distracted by the lovely sway in her near naked ass as she strode through the open space.

*Pick your poison, Reilly. The woman or the job, but you can't do both at once.*

Heather poked her head out from the dressing room. "I'm going to change, unless you have any objections."

Callum objected, but for personal reasons.

"Go ahead," he said. "I'll wait."

He leaned against the doorjamb.

"What's on the second and third floors?"

"Don't know," Heather said through the door. "Master William said they needed too much work to make it worth his while to renovate and rent."

"In New York, with the premium on real estate?"

"Maybe he just wanted his privacy," she said. "But you'd have to ask him."

"If I can find him. Do you think there is a secret way out of the building?"

"Oh, for heaven's sake." The door opened and Heather stood there with an incredulous expression.

"I mean," Callum said, "don't you find it odd that the owner of the club disappeared when there was a fire alarm pulled? Wouldn't he be here to protect his assets?"

"I'm sure that he got a call from his wife and went home before the commotion started. Occam's Razor, Reilly."

"Excuse me?"

"The simplest solution is the answer."

"I know what Occam's Razor is."

Heather tossed a rueful smile over her shoulder, then looked at her phone and entered the dressing room. She returned and pushed bags, sweaters and a heap of other clothes at him.

"Hold these. I'll lock the back door and we'll exit the front where I can lock it with the security code."

Before he could answer, Heather trotted toward the back, and Callum stood with his overburdened arms waiting for her return. It occurred to him that in the one act of handing him the patrons' belongings, she made sure that he could do little but hold or drop them. Heather hobbled him with the clothing and made it impossible for him to act aggressively without communicating his intentions.

*Because a man kneeling at your feet can't kick you in the teeth.*

What a statement. Who kicked her in the teeth? Who'd want to hurt Heather? Some sick asshole. A spark of anger lit in his heart. If he found anyone that had or would hurt Heather, he'd —he'd—what?

*The woman is proficient with whips. She doesn't need your help.*

Had Callum had ever met a woman that didn't need a man's protection? He had known a few female soldiers overseas, but as tough as they were, they were constantly on guard against the overly persistent attentions of soldiers too far from home with few pleasures. Heather, however, didn't seem on guard. She appeared to be in charge at all times.

To his surprise, Callum found that quality hot.

Heather returned within a minute and with a nod of her head directed him to the door so they stood outside the club. Different members crowded around them, and Heather handed off the items. As Callum's burden grew lighter, he watched her and how she interacted with the club patrons. Yep, there was no question who commanded this scene. Patrons thanked her and moved off as the firefighters and the police left the scene.

Emmons walked to him.

"Find anything missing?"

Callum shook his head. "No. Miss Skye said there was nothing missing."

"Except the club owner. Miss Skye, do you know where the club owner lives so we can talk to him? We checked the address on his driver's license, but a resident says he doesn't live there anymore."

"He and his wife just moved into a new apartment in the Upper East Side. I'll give you the address."

While Heather talked with Emmons, Master Paul approached Callum.

"Find anything in there?"

Callum shook his head. There was nothing to find, and no leads to go on, just like his entire year in New York. It was time to pack it in for the night and start again tomorrow.

"Just many questions."

Paul raised an eyebrow. "Can you escort Miss Heather home? I'm concerned. Any sub needs more time than she had to level out."

"She seems fine," Callum said. "But I'll make sure she gets home okay."

"Thanks. Stop by the bar sometime for a drink."

"Sure."

Heather turned back to them as Emmons walked away.

"Good night, you two," Master Paul said.

"You're leaving?" Heather said.

"You're in good hands, Mistress Heather," Paul said. "Don't

do anything I wouldn't, which isn't that much." He winked at them and then sauntered toward the street.

"What does he mean by that?" Heather said.

Callum frowned. "Don't know, but I'll escort you home."

Heather shook her head. "Why on earth would you do that?"

Callum looked into Heather's gorgeous emerald eyes and could think of only one answer to that question. He stepped forward and kissed her.

## 12

Callum's lips sizzled, sending sparks up Heather's spine. Heather melted against his body, and the only thing that existed was his touch. His hard body incited ideas of getting as close to it as possible, and she opened her mouth to deepen the kiss. His intoxicating taste made her want to lick him in as many places as possible. Her breathing revved fast as she barreled toward the edge of fainting. What was it about this man that made her lose her mind?

Heather wanted to sink to her knees and press her lips against his crotch. She imagined his sexy scent overwhelming her sense, so she'd beg to taste him. And that thought shocked her. No way would she ever put herself in a sub position to a man.

She pushed away and stepped back.

"Don't do that again," she said. Heather tried for her Domme's voice but found it strangled in her throat, and instead it sounded weak and unsure.

"Heather, what's wrong?"

"You! You're not the type of man I want."

"A submissive man," he sighed.

"Yes."

His eyes glittered as he searched her face. Then the corner of his mouth rose before Callum spoke.

"Because a real man scares you all to hell."

Heather's eyes widened, and she drew her hand back and smashed her palm across his jaw. Callum's eyebrows flew up as he stepped backward and rubbed his jaw.

"Whatever, Callum Reilly. Don't bother me again."

Heather turned smartly on her stilettos and walked toward the street. She'd catch the subway to get to her apartment, or rather Aaron's apartment she sublet. With the way Callum Reilly seemed to follow her around, she shouldn't go home yet. Heather wanted to check in on Master William and Samantha and let him know about the incident at the club.

She walked across the street to Master Paul's bar, the Onion and Olive, and turned right on the parallel road to where cabbies picked up fairs. If she was lucky, there would be a cab waiting for a fare, and if she wasn't, she'd enter the bar for a drink. Though not much of a drinker, she needed some liquid fortification now.

But Heather was in luck as a Yellow Cab pulled into the taxi stand. She knocked on the door and the driver lowered the back window. "Looking for a fare?" she said. "I want to get to the Upper East Side."

The cabbie's eyes lit up at the mention of a high-income area fare. She supposed the driver believed she was rich, but she didn't care.

Heather gave the cabbie the address and slid her business credit card in the slot.

The driver jerked the car into the lane, a move that no daytime driver would try because of congestion.

"Hey," she complained.

"You want to drive your car? Or ride in mine?"

Heather folded her arms and sunk into the seat. She still shivered because despite her brave front, getting jolted without warning from subspace fried her nerves. It ticked off Heather that her good time got uninterrupted. Plus, resentment curled in her stomach for Callum kissing her without permission. Yes, in the vanilla world, that could, and frequently did, happen, but Heather wasn't vanilla and would never accept that behavior from a man.

Could she?

Callum differed from any man she had met, or at least her reaction to him was unlike her usual experience. Neither Dom nor sub got her motor running the way Callum Reilly did. The thought of sinking to her knees to kiss his erection through his pants fueled different unbidden fantasies, a few of which involved calling him "sir."

And this distressed her. No way would she bow to any man.

The cab stopped at Master William's address and she exited with a quick thanks to the cab driver, then she entered the atrium of the thirty-floor building. A doorman stood behind a curved desk.

"Excuse me," he said. "You are looking for who?"

"William and Samantha Ianucci. I'm a friend of theirs."

"And your name?"

"Heather Skye."

The doorman gave her leather outfit the once-over and his mouth quirked in disapproval. What sort of stuck-up place was this?

"I'll ring their apartment."

He picked up a handset, and after a long minute, spoke into it.

"You can go up, miss, to apartment 2901. Mrs. Ianucci is at home."

Samantha, but not William? Heather did not expect this, and the hair on the back of her neck rose.

"Hello!" Samantha said as she threw open the door and gave Heather a hug. "I've been alone for hours. Lexi's husband finally threw me out saying he wanted time alone with his wife before the baby came, and I'm absolutely at ends. Do you want a drink?"

"A ginger ale if you have it."

Heather walked and gazed at the large living room with its high ceilings, and followed Samantha to the kitchen equipped with top-of-the-line appliances and spacious marble countertops.

"Nice place."

"I'm still decorating, but honestly, now I understand why people hire decorators. It's going to take me forever to get this place feeling homey."

"So William isn't home?"

"No. He's at the club, where I thought you'd be." Samantha handed Heather a ginger ale with ice.

Heather shook her head. "No. Gabriel Russo showed up. Do you know him?"

Samantha frowned. "Yes, Uncle Gitchy."

"Your face tells me you don't like him."

"I don't approve of what he's into. William has done what he could to cut ties, but Gitchy keeps showing up. And you say he was at the club."

"I'm afraid so. And then he and William disappeared around the time someone pulled the fire alarm to the club, making us empty it."

"Fire alarm? Was there a fire? Any damage?"

"No. But Master Paul thought it was a good idea to close the club for the night."

Samantha sighed. "Paul was probably right. Hold on. I'll call William's sister and see if she knows anything."

Her hostess walked out of the kitchen, and from the next room, Samantha's hushed voice wafted into the living room. Heather didn't catch all the words, but Samantha's voice sounded stressed.

Samantha returned and wore a worried expression.

"Well, no one has called her, and since the club is closer to his parents' building than here, you would think he might stop there."

"I should get going."

"No, stay. We haven't hung out together since the baby shower."

"Another time, Samantha."

"Good to see you. Let's do a girls' night out sometime soon."

"Sounds fun. While we're at it, we'll drag my soon-to-be roommate with us."

"Yeah, when are you moving there?"

"When the landlord slaps on a fresh coat of paint."

"Oh, yeah, that guy. Who thinks a New York minute equates with California dreaming. I remember him."

"When was the last time it got painted? In the '90s?"

"Seems like it. I hope it brings you as much luck as Lexi and me."

"How's that?"

"We both met our guys while living in that apartment."

"You mean your rich and incredibly sexy guys."

"Exactly!"

"Ha. No rich guys for me. When you see William, tell him we shut up the club and why."

"I will. Thanks for coming by, Heather."

"Good night."

Samantha closed the door with a perplexed expression on her face, and Heather did not blame her. William Ianucci valued dependability and discipline, and if he didn't return to his apartment, something had perturbed his carefully crafted schedule.

And that had to be the mysterious Gabriel Russo.

Though it went against her New Yorker's grain, she hailed another cab. She wasn't far from her apartment and could walk a few blocks. This part of the city was safe. But she couldn't shake the feeling that something was massively wrong, so she told the cabbie to take her back to the club.

It was as dark as she left it, and she wondered what had gotten into her. Callum's questions about the upper floors and a secret entrance to New York's labyrinthine underground system haunted her. Abandoned, except for homeless "mole people" who used it for shelter or taggers to spray their graffiti and not get arrested, the abandoned subway corridors weren't a place that most people dared to venture.

Would William? And why?

Samantha used her security code to unlock the door and stepped inside the dark atrium of *La Corda Rosa*. She flicked on the lights to a banging noise and swearing.

"Who's there?" she said.

Silence.

Swallowing hard, she stepped forward.

"Whoever's here, if you don't answer, I'm calling the police."

"Don't," a familiar voice said.

Heather huffed. "Reilly, what the hell are you doing in here?"

Callum stepped forward from the back of the club and stepped onto the hardwood floor of the empty exhibition area.

"Investigating," he said.

She put her hands on her hips. "In your capacity as a police officer? Do you have a warrant?"

Callum looked away. "No."

"Then get out!"

"Look, no one can find Ianucci. I think something happened to him."

"And why is this of great interest to you, Reilly?"

"Because William Ianucci's family is part of the New York mob scene and has been for a least a hundred years."

"You're ridiculous. I've known him for ten years and never saw an inkling of connections to organized crime."

"Do you think he'd tell you? Gabriel Russo is a close associate of the Ianucci family, and he's connected to Augustine Nicero, a prominent New York crime boss."

Samantha huffed again with annoyance. "I've never seen Gabriel Russo before today, and I've never heard of Augustine Nicero. I don't know what game you are playing, Detective Reilly, but you need to leave now before I report you to your superiors."

Callum's eyes narrowed.

"Fine, I'll—"

But then a noise at the back of the building made both of them turn their heads. Callum drew a handgun from inside his jacket and signaled for her to keep quiet and stay where she was. She stared into the murky back half of the club, which had muted lighting for atmosphere, and only saw Callum in shadow, walking in measured paces.

"Omph!" she heard, and then the scuffle of two people fighting. Her heart raced as the fighting continued, and she worried that Callum was hurt. She edged toward the Spanking Room, the first door on the left, and cracked open the door and reached in, and pulled a bullwhip off the wall as a weapon.

"Hands behind your head!" Callum said. The click of handcuffs told her Callum had secured the intruder.

"Callum! Are you okay?"

"Fine. Bastard knocked the gun out of my hand in a lucky shot. Don't get cocky, asshole. You're going to the station."

"Where did he come from? The backdoor was locked."

Heather switched on an overhead light to reveal Callum pulling a red-haired man to his feet.

"Nope. Someone put a matchbook in the lock. Stop resisting, asshole. Heather, call the police and tell them you found an intruder. Hey, jerk, have you seen William Ianucci?"

"I'm looking for him myself."

Callum glared at the man. "Why?"

The man's mouth drew a hard line.

"Fine. You sort it out at the precinct. Heather?"

"Now, go, Callum."

"You sure?"

Heather cracked the whip on the floor and the man's eyes went wide. Callum's mouth upturned in a smile.

"Yeah, you better go, Callum, before I report you, too."

"You calling the police?"

"Don't worry about that, Callum."

"I want those cuffs back," Callum said before he slipped out of the back door.

Heather took out her keys and made sure it was locked. Then she fingered her handcuff keys and walked to the man and held them so the man could see them.

"Who are you?"

"Phil Praegano."

"And you are who to William Ianucci?"

"Our families ran crews for the same guys until Ianucci got out last year."

Heather stared at Praegano. Last year? William had been part of organized crime all the time she knew him? The notion shocked Heather. Krystal and she had avoided any type of illegal activity since Krystal had an arrest warrant out on her. And both were associated with a man involved in crime?

"And why are you here?"

"I wanted to warn him that the Feds are investigating him, but I guess since you are hanging out with a Fed you know that already."

## 13

### CALLUM

HEATHER LOOKED SO HOT WITH THE WHIP IN HER HAND, CALLUM didn't want to leave her behind in the club. But he believed her when she said she would report him to the precinct, which would get to his captain, who did not need that kind of trouble.

Still, he wanted to discover who the hell the guy was that had broken into *La Corda Rosa*. The question lit his brain so much he didn't want to return to his hotel. He should, but if he did, he'd go home alone once more.

And that thought sucked.

For the first time in many years, Callum didn't want to crawl into bed alone and spend another sleepless night trying to figure an angle that would solve this case.

His phone rang as he walked the New York streets lit by street lamps and neon signs.

"Reilly," he said.

"It's Aaron. I'm just checking if you want my old apartment. Because if you don't, then I'll have to look in other places. I understand Heather will move into her new digs within a month."

Hell. Callum hated leaving a buddy up in the air, but it wasn't like he seriously considered taking the apartment.

"Tell you what. I'll drop off a check to cover the rest of the lease. We'll worry about when Heather moves out later."

"You sure?"

Why did he speak so quickly?

*You're just helping a friend.*

Callum's salary as an NCIS agent was more than generous for his needs. Callum banked most of his pay when he worked overseas. Notwithstanding his unused trust fund, he had more than enough money to pay for the apartment. It wouldn't hurt to spend his hoard to give Aaron a hand.

"Dude, all my money from working the Sandbox is still in the bank. Trust me. I'm good."

"No doubt. That's why I asked you. Thanks, buddy."

It was the least he could do for one of his best friends in the world, who he barely paid attention to in New York because of work. If Aaron wasn't so busy with his new family, Callum was sure Aaron would extend more invites to hang out.

Still, having a friend, someone he could count on, a person with a quiet, normal life, seemed a rare comfort for Callum. While he had buddies in the service, you couldn't count on someone being there, because of the high risk of injury or death. It was always a shock to learn that someone you played poker with the previous night got his life cut short in the morning.

He looked ahead at the city street as he headed for the precinct. It was always the same, and despite being New York, much safer than a war zone dealing with insurgents, or worse, the Merchants of Death that preyed on those insurgents to make a buck. Red Tide was one such organization, and now they'd reached their tentacles into the United States and New York, and he had to stop them.

Otherwise, the gruesome death of his informant would go unavenged.

Callum shook his head. From where did these thoughts emerge? He had one purpose. Find the people laundering money for Red Tide and arrest them. And he was no closer to that than the first day he arrived in New York.

Soon he reached the precinct and entered the 19th-century building. The police station was the worse for wear, with the varnish of the hardwood floors worn from so many people treading it. The wood frames and molding had been painted over so many times that the green paint peeled just, he swore, from looking at it.

The sergeant at the desk looked up.

"Reilly, what the hell are you doing here at this time of night?"

"I'm checking on something, Sergeant Sloan. Is there a report of an intruder at *La Corda Rosa*?"

"Let me check."

Sloan typed into his computer and his mouth quirked.

"When would this be?"

"Within an hour. Nothing?"

"No."

He pulled out his phone and called Heather while his heart curdled with worry. He shouldn't have left her with that criminal, no matter what she said.

"This is Heather."

"It's me. Callum."

"Yeah, I saw your mug on my phone. I was just getting ready to change your name from Detective Reilly to 'dickhead.'"

Callum rubbed his forehead. How the hell did he tick her off this time?

"Heather, are you okay? You didn't call the police on the man that broke into *La Corda Rosa*."

"What man?" Heather spoke with an innocent tone to her voice.

"What game are you playing, Heather? If you aren't okay, then I'll come over right now."

"Try it and I'll have you arrested for trespassing, like I should have when you first showed up. Now, stop bothering me, Detective, or I will report you to your superiors."

Heather clicked off the call abruptly, and Callum stood staring at his phone as if it would give him answers to Heather's behavior. But it wouldn't.

What the hell happened? Why didn't she report the trespasser?

Callum's stomach churned with the sort of sensations he had when on assignment in the Sandbox and things were about to blow up figuratively, or literally. It was the same sort of feeling he had when his Afghani informant Aidila walked away that last time saying, "Don't worry, Reilly. I will not be harmed." He sensed that Heather had or was about to get into big trouble. Despite her admonishment to stay away, he couldn't stand the thought of Heather facing danger.

He'd rather she file a complaint on him than allow her to get hurt.

Callum pivoted and strode from the station house, with Sergeant Sloan calling after him. Outside, he ran, hoping that Heather hadn't yet left the club. His feet pounded the pavement as he picked up the pace while the sense of impending doom grew.

As he reached the corner with the Onion and Olive, he caught a flash of Heather's magenta-edged hair across the street as she walked toward a cab.

"Heather!" he called.

But she didn't glance his way. Instead, she opened the cab's door and stepped inside.

He sprinted across the street, and after reaching the cab, yanked at the handle.

"Hey, buddy," yelled the cabbie.

Callum held up his badge. "NYPD," he said.

The cabbie rolled down his window.

"What do you want?"

"Just go," Heather said. "This man has been harassing me."

"Sorry, miss. I'm not getting in trouble with the police. You can step out, or settle this with him."

Callum bent and stuck his head inside the open window.

"Heather, I'm coming with you."

Heather's gorgeous face filled with outrage. "Are you nuts?"

"You got information from that guy, and you're about to do something stupid."

"How would you know that?"

"From years of doing stupid things just like this. Let me in, Heather. I just want to help you."

"Says the man that's lied to me every step of the way."

"Feed the meter," the cabbie said, "or get the hell out."

"What do you mean lie?"

"So you aren't a Federal agent?"

Oh, hell. Who the hell told her that? Had to be that guy at the club. Now, Callum's sense of danger spiked. If his real identity was revealed to the New York mob, not just Heather, he was in deep trouble.

"That's on a need-to-know basis."

"Folks," the cabbie said. "I don't work for free."

Callum pulled out his wallet and tossed a fifty on the front seat. "That should buy me a few minutes, right?"

The cabbie grumbled, but turned on the meter.

"Need to know? That's a laugh," Heather said. "Don't you think I needed that honesty of who the hell you were before you kissed me?"

"Whoa," the cabbie said. "This is better than a telenovela show."

"Shut up," Heather said testily.

"Hey, I don't have to stand that kind of talk," replied the cabbie.

"Heather, let me get in, and I'll explain everything."

"Why should I? You've been spying on me and my friends. Why? What nefarious things do you think we are doing?"

"Not you. I wasn't spying on you."

"So who? Master William?"

"Whoa," the cabbie said. "Master? What sort of freaky things are you into, lady?"

"Will you just move the cab already? Do it before I report you to your cab company."

"Don't worry about her," Callum said. "She threatens to report everyone."

Heather scoffed, crossed her arms, and glared at Callum.

A phone rang, and the cabbie answered it.

"Yeah. No. I have a fare. The meter is running. I know I'm not moving. A man and woman are talking. Yeah. It sounds crazy to me, too. I'll call you when I'm clear." The cabbie sighed. "Either we move or you guys get out. I'm not supposed to stand in the street if it's not a taxi stand."

"Fine," Heather said. "Let him in."

The locks clicked open, and Callum slid in next to Heather.

"Where to, lady?"

Heather gave him the Little Italy address of Jimmy Mack's Smoke Shop.

Callum sucked in a breath. Why would she go there? Callum had arrested Jimmy Mack, but he was out in a matter of hours after he called his lawyer. Bookmaking was a felony in New York, but Callum had found out quickly the other people he arrested in the shop lost their memory and/or their ability to speak. Suddenly there was no one, except Matheson, who accompanied him, to corroborate what was said that gave Callum probable cause to rush into the back room. "Why are you going there?"

"Phil Praegano said that Gabriel Russo may have taken Master William there."

"Heather, you know he's a gang boss, right?"

"Master William? I don't think so." Heather shot him a piercing glance that communicated that she did not believe Callum.

"I mean Jimmy Mack."

"Reilly, what planet do you come from? Crime bosses are nothing new in New York City. And most keep low profiles and just do their business."

"Their illegal business."

"There are people who thought what I did was illegal. They called it prostitution even though I didn't sell sex. Maybe this whole legal, illegal thing is a matter of perception."

Callum snorted. "I'm pretty sure it's a matter of the law."

"You would look at it that way. That's what makes it so easy for you to lie to people that befriend you. Doesn't it bother you that the people who uphold the law, such as detectives and lawyers, are professional liars?"

"Okay, you two. Here's your destination. Out."

Callum shook his head. He had no intention of letting Heather walk into danger. He wanted her to stay in the cab while he checked things out. "There's another fifty in it for you if you sit with the meter running—"

"Whatever you two have going, I want no part of it. I've got another fare I need to get to. Goodbye."

"Come on, Reilly. Let's get this over with."

After they exited, the cab rushed off.

"I guess," Heather said, "the talk about crime bosses made him rethink our fare."

Callum quirked his mouth. "Probably smarter than both of us."

"So what's your plan, Reilly?"

"What did you plan?"

"I thought I'd find their front door and knock on it. Say I was looking for Jimmy Mack—that we had some business."

"It has the virtue of simplicity. But what makes you think that Jimmy Mack will tell you anything?"

"Men naturally drop their guard around me."

"I believe you. But this is far too dangerous for a civilian. You stay here, and I'll walk around the building and see if there is an entrance. Jimmy Mack's parents own this building. That could mean they or he have apartments on the other floors."

"That would be Little Italy, for sure. But I'm not standing here on the street in the middle of the night while you traipse around the building."

Callum looked away, but he agreed inwardly that she shouldn't stand on the street outside a gangster's place of business.

"Okay, but stay five steps behind me. And if I tell you to run, you do it."

## 14

"I don't believe you," Heather said as she followed Callum, the liar, down an alley strewn with garbage and empty boxes. At the opposite end of the open alleyway, a stinking dumpster sat.

"What?" he said distractedly. Callum peered into the half-lit alley before them.

"About Master William being involved in organized crime. I've known him too long."

"How long have you known him?"

"Ten years. He trained me as a Domme. And in all that time, I've never seen him do anything illegal. He blew up when someone brought alcohol into the club one time. The club doesn't have a liquor license, and he could have gotten into trouble."

Callum kept his back to her, but he spoke loudly enough for her to hear.

"That only tells me he likes to keep a low profile."

"When you run a BDSM club, you do that. Cops still run vice operations. But you wouldn't know that, would you, Mr. Federal Agent?"

"And how did you meet Ianucci?"

"I answered an ad for submissives."

Callum snorted as he stepped forward. "Of course you did."

Heather put her hands on her hips. "What does that mean?"

Callum whirled. "Look, I don't understand the level of BDSM in which you engage."

"Engage? I use the word 'play.'"

"Use whatever word you like. I still don't understand it. I don't understand men wanting to get whipped or women wanting to get tied up. Where I come from, people get tortured in those ways."

Heather stared at Callum. "Where do you come from?"

Callum's jaw set, and he turned away. "Forget I said that."

"I gather you're doing some undercover thing. And you're investigating Master William for God-knows-what. There is no need to go James Bond on me and play coy."

"Ssh," he said. "Here's the door."

Callum stood at a brown door painted so many times that the chips had chips in them. He turned the handle with aching slowness, but it wouldn't open.

"Damn," he whispered.

The door's lock clicked. Callum grabbed her arm and dragged her to the opposite side of the dumpster. She glared at him but kept quiet as the door swung open with a creak. Heather caught the distinct smell of tobacco.

"What do you think the boss will do with him?" one man said.

"Someone cooperating with the cops? What do you think happens?"

"Get in here, you two," a harsher voice said.

The door slammed shut, and Heather glanced at Callum, who peeked around the corner with a grim expression on his face.

"Do you think—"Heather said.

But Callum held up his hand, signaling her not to speak. She huffed and fell back against the brick wall.

*What will happen now?*

Was Master William in that building? Did those men intend to harm him?

"You stay here," Callum said.

"Wait—"

But Callum disappeared around the corner, leaving her alone.

The lack of near traffic noise was eerie. In the distance, a siren cut through the night but sounded like it moved away, not closer.

*What the hell do I do now?*

Heather crossed her arms and pursed her lips as she listened to the sounds of New York at night. Cars whooshed by at either end of the alley. Classical music wafted from someone's open window. Then she heard rustling behind the sour-smelling dumpster, and a rat scurried from between the container and the wall.

She shrieked in surprise.

*Damn rodents. Curse of the city.*

The back door opened suddenly, and a short, rotund man stepped out.

"Who the hell are you?" he asked.

"Um, I need to see Jimmy Mack."

The man's eyes narrowed. Then his eyes fell on her outfit of a corset, short leather skirt, and handmade thigh-high leather boots. He sneered, and he shouldn't have. Heather had stuck a bullwhip in the back of her corset.

"Didn't know Jimmy Mack went for your type." Sleaze oozed from his mouth when he spoke.

She met his eyes dead-on. "You don't know the type of woman I am."

And if the creep found out, he'd regret it.

This man, dressed in cheap clothes to which clung the odor of his last pizza slice, didn't frighten Heather. And he needed a lesson in respect from Mr. Bullwhip.

"Well, get inside. I'm not supposed to leave the door open."

Heather walked forward into the hallway. A single ceiling fixture lit the hallway. A disgusting miasma of stale cigarettes, ancient enamel paint, and the funk of mold-infested walls wafted in the air.

"Get moving," the man said behind her.

"Gladly," she said under her breath. The sooner she left this building, the better for her health.

With the creep behind her, she strode through the hallway with the sharp sound of her high heels clicking on the wood floorboards. They came to a wide doorway where Heather spotted men at desks working a phone bank.

"What—" another deeper voice said. A portly man dressed in a polo shirt and khakis stepped forward. "What is this, *stunad*? Who is this woman, and why is she here?"

"She said she had business with you."

Jimmy Mack's eyes traveled her lithe body.

"What do you want?"

"Is there a place to talk?"

"This is where we talk. Who the hell are you?"

"I'm Heather Skye. I'm an associate of William Ianucci."

"Associate? Oh, you're from that club of his." Jimmy Mack spoke flatly, without a kernel of interest in his voice.

"I'm a member," she said.

"Fine. Then leave now."

"I'm looking for William. Gabriel Russo was with him."

Jimmy Mack spit on the floor. "Russo," he said disparagingly. "If Ianucci was with him, he might not be coming back."

"What? Why?"

"Get out of here. I'm not talking about family business with you. Guido," he snapped. "Show the lady out."

Guido put his hands on her arm, but she shook it off.

"Where can I find Russo?" She narrowed her eyes and stared down Jimmy Mack as she would a sub, calling on all her Domme presence to show that man who was boss. Jimmy Mack stepped back involuntarily and then shook his head as if to snap himself out of Heather's spell.

"I'm not the one to ask. And the one you could ask wouldn't talk to you. So now, get out of my shop, lady, and don't come back. This is no place for you."

Jimmy Mack glared at her, and Heather could see from his steely gaze that she'd get no more from him,.

"Thank you, Mr. Mack. But if you hear something, contact me at Shop BIO. I'll make it worth your while."

"Shop BIO? What kind of place is that?"

"I make and sell leather goods, like what you see on me now. I'm sure you know some woman that would like a nice pair of boots like these."

Jimmy Mack eyed her boots.

"Custom work?"

"The best."

"I'll think about it, Miss Skye. Now, don't let the door hit your lovely ass on the way out."

He sneered the last words, and Heather got the message. She had worn out her very brief welcome.

"Thank you for the lovely chat," she said. Heather gave him one last condescending glance and walked with a sway down the hall toward the back door. She'd learned little, but then she didn't think Master William was in this building. Jimmy Mack would be a man used to lying, but she saw in his face that he didn't lie to her. Heather was very astute at telling when men lied.

*Except for Callum.*

What was it about the man that made her ignore all the danger signs? He was not her type of man, she suspected that he tried to cultivate a relationship with her as an excuse to spend more time at the club, and the biggie—Callum lied to her about who he was.

And he still wasn't being straight with her.

Heather stepped into the alleyway. When the door shut behind her with a thud, she turned with hands on hips, searching for Callum.

What the hell would she do with him?

"Heather! Thank God! Where did you go?"

"Nowhere. I tired of waiting around and walked around the block. Did you see anything helpful?"

"No. The windows are painted black on the first floor."

"Good. Then I'm going home." Heather hurried down the alley before he could try to talk her out of leaving.

But he followed, double-timing his step to catch up with her.

"Wait up, Heather."

Heather reached the curb and scanned the street both ways for a taxi. One shot by her, ignoring her hand wave. Callum reached her, and she did her best to ignore him.

"Hey, where are you going?" he said.

"Home," she said frostily. Another taxi sped by, and she swore.

"Here," he said. Callum stepped into the street and flagged a taxi, who pulled to the curb.

Heather slid into the cab, but before she could stop him, he plopped into the seat next to her. She glared at him.

"You don't mind sharing a cab with me, right?"

She rolled her eyes. "I can't stop you."

"Where to?" the cabbie said.

"Upper East Side. You can drop him off wherever he wants to

go after." Heather gave the cabbie the address while Callum checked his phone. He pursed his lips, then slipped it into his jeans pocket.

"Why are you angry at me?" he said.

Heather scoffed. "Me angry? You'd be so lucky. Right now, I despise you, Reilly, or whatever your name is."

"It's Reilly."

"So you told the truth about one thing. Big deal. What were you trying to do skulking around my friends and *La Corda Rosa*?"

Callum looked out the window.

"That's classified," he said grimly.

"Right. Hide behind military secrets. Pretend to be interested in my world. My friends. Spying on people who've only shown you kindness."

Callum folded his arms, snorted, and continued to look out the window.

"Aren't you going to answer me?" she said. Heather pitched her voice in the demanding tone that made submissive men shiver. But Callum only gave her a bored glance.

"Maybe that voice thing you have going on works with the men you whip, but it doesn't work with me. People have trained me who could make your skin melt just from them addressing you by name and rank."

Heather gave Callum a hard stare. She had judged him to be a dominant, and this only proved it. Like all dominants, Callum had a low need for approval from other people and had high self-esteem. He was correct. Her Domme persona would not work on him.

And that grated against her Domme personality and pinged her sense that he had betrayed her. And that bothered her, though it shouldn't. So why should she care about Callum Reilly?

*Because he's the hottest thing on two legs that you've seen in a decade.*

God, she hated that thought.

Heather huffed.

"Oh, well, if you're that much of a hard-ass, by all means, continue on your secret mission. Only you won't be doing it at *La Corda Rosa* anymore."

Callum rubbed his forehead, and one corner of his mouth twitched.

"Okay, Heather. You win. I don't want to admit this, but I need your help. Someone involved in the New York organized crime is laundering money for a terrorist organization."

"Who?"

"I thought, and I still do, William Ianucci."

Heather crossed her arms. "That's ridiculous."

"Think about it. Ianucci has a business where he can list anyone as a member, ascribe any amount of money to client services, and who would be the wiser? It's not like there is a money model for BDSM clubs like there is for other businesses, so there is no way to check if the income he reports from it is reasonable. It's a business ripe for money laundering."

"That proves nothing."

"Heather, you told me that William invested in your business. From your Midtown address, I assume it was a sizeable amount of money."

"Well, a half a million, but we make our payments each month."

"Exactly, Heather. And how many other businesses has he done that with? He's been expanding his restaurant empire, right? Again, another place to pass through large amounts of cash."

"Doing business is not a crime. And two restaurants are hardly an empire."

"But supporting terrorist activities is."

Heather shook her head. "You've got this all wrong, Callum."

"No, I don't."

"Okay, then. Cabbie, turn around, go back two blocks." She gave the driver another address.

"What?" Callum said.

"There is one person we can ask, and I'm sure she'll give us straight answers."

"Who?"

"His wife, Samantha Ianucci."

## 15

HEATHER WALKED INTO IANUCCI'S APARTMENT BUILDING AS IF SHE owned it. Callum admitted that he found Heather's self-confidence intoxicating. He had never met a woman like her, and he doubted he'd meet another.

*That's one woman that wouldn't pass muster back home.*

A woman like Heather was not in Callum's family's wheelhouse. With her magenta-tipped hair, face piercings, and her body-tight leather wardrobe, his ultra-conservative father would conclude unsavory things about her. He most definitely would not invite her to dinner at the country club, and he would not introduce Heather as his girlfriend.

As if he could get so lucky.

He could imagine his father's disapproving expression and the man's offer to put up Heather at a moderately priced local hotel instead of offering her a room in their fourteen-room mansion. And he also imagined Heather raking his father with her appraising Domme's eyes and making him squirm.

"Let's go, Callum," she would say. "I understand what you mean now. We'll come back another time."

And she'd do it without offering a single insult, with total composure.

The Ianuccis' doorman didn't look pleased to see her either. Still, he called their apartment and then waved Heather and Callum toward the elevator. Callum gave the man a twenty to generate goodwill, though the doorman stared dismissively at the bill.

"Reilly," Heather said before she entered the elevator. Callum followed, and he noted the floor number she pressed. Watching people and his environment was a habit Callum couldn't turn off. He was 6,800 miles from Kabul, but it seemed only a street away.

The elevator opened in a hall, and a door cracked opened. A woman with short-cropped but curly hair stood in the doorway.

"Heather? Do you have news of William?"

"You haven't heard from him either?"

"No, and I'm getting worried. William would have called by now."

"Samantha, this is Callum Reilly."

Samantha Ianucci gave him a warm smile.

"Hello, Mr. Reilly. William spoke of you."

Heather spoke up. "Can we come in, Samantha? We need to speak with you. Before you say yes, Callum is Detective Reilly, working with the NYPD, but also a Federal agency."

"NCIS, ma'am."

Samantha stared at Callum as if she hadn't seen him before, and she sucked in a breath as if steeling herself for the worst.

"You can come in, but don't call me ma'am. You make me feel old."

"Not my intention, Mrs. Ianucci."

Samantha frowned. "That's worse. Mrs. Ianucci is William's mother. Call me Sam or Samantha. And come in." She waved them inside, and Callum looked around the spacious apartment, which appeared recently remodeled. Floor-to-ceiling windows joined at a corner looking over the city and the south end of Central Park. The white marble floors held a high glass-like polish, and to the left, a large white marble-topped island separated the living room and kitchen area. A hallway ran perpendicular to the kitchen area, but the hallway was dark so that Callum couldn't see down it.

"You have a lovely home."

"I still have a lot of work to do to make it home, but it's big enough for a family, so that's one project." She led them to the oversized red L-shaped couch positioned to capture the view at both large windows. A conical gas fireplace, lit with dancing flames, sat in the corner. "Can I get you something to drink? If we were in William's mother's house, she'd have a six-course dinner on the table already and act highly offended if you didn't eat. You're lucky all I have is water, soda, and wine."

"None for me," Heather said.

"I'm good," Callum said.

Heather shot him a glance that said he was anything but.

Samantha folded her hands in her lap and glanced first at Heather, then Callum. "What can I do for you?"

Heather sighed. "There is no easy way to say this, Samantha. Detective—"

"Special Agent," Callum said.

Heather shot another glare at Callum.

"Okay, then, Special Agent Reilly thinks William is involved with organized crime."

Samantha nodded.

She said, "At one time, his whole family."

Callum raised his eyebrows, surprised at Samantha's easy confession.

"William didn't take part in the family business. And he thought and still does that there was no need for the family to stay involved in illegal activities. He had already made his first billion through the restaurant, in real estate, and the club. But *La Familia* didn't want to let go. So William made a deal with Augustine Nicero. Do you know him?"

"Yes," Callum said. "He's the boss of the Nicero crime family."

"That's right. William made a deal to get the Ianucci family out. They were never big fishes, anyway. And there were, um, problems that I've been sworn not to discuss, so Nicero let the Ianuccis out."

Callum leaned over his knees and steepled his fingers.

"That's a very unusual story."

"My William is a very unusual man." Samantha smiled. "Special Agent, if you think William is involved with illegal activities, you are wrong. I wouldn't stay with him if he were."

"What about any of his family?"

"Same thing. William's parents are very relieved. They don't have to worry about their children, and they are looking forward to grandchildren who will have a brighter future. And William makes sure that everyone is taken care of well. With interest from his different investments, as you can see, we live well."

"So you're telling me that your husband does not need money? And he has no desire or need to work in organized crime?"

"If you doubt me, check out his finances. You'll see everything I've said is true."

"And yet, Gabriel Russo showed up at *La Corda Rosa* tonight."

Samantha pursed her lips.

"I don't know why, but he's an old family friend."

"As well as being an associate of the Nicero Crime family," Callum said.

"William is no longer a part of that." Ianucci's wife's eyes narrowed, and Callum thought they were close to getting thrown out.

"And you do not know where your husband is—"

Heather's phone rang, and she pulled from inside her corset. Callum pursed his lips and looked away because he shouldn't stare. But God, he wanted to.

"It's Aaron," she announced. "Why would he call? Excuse me."

"Hey, Aaron," she said. "No, I haven't been to the apartment all day. Really? Anything taken? No, I only have clothes there. The rest is in storage. Okay, thanks for telling me." She clicked off the call and glared at Callum.

"Okay, Special Agent Reilly, does that answer your questions?" Heather said.

"Well—"

"Then let's go. Samantha, I promise if I hear anything, I'll call you."

"Same, Heather. Thanks for dropping by. Nice meeting you, Special Agent."

When the doors to the elevator closed, Callum turned to Heather.

"Why did you do that? I hadn't finished questioning her."

"You mean interrogating her. And I won't have it. She's my friend, and she's going through enough without you accusing her husband of committing crimes."

Heather's disapproving expression was full of heat—in fact blazing hot. Callum imagined kissing the frown from her gorgeous face, and his cock tingled at the thought.

*It's crazy how much this woman turns me on.*

"What was the call from Aaron about?"

"He got a message from the super that someone broke into the apartment. The police took the report and left."

Immediately, Callum straightened and scanned the street for any suspicious persons.

"Did they take anything obvious, TV, computer, iPad?"

"The TV is still there. I keep my computer in the store. Wait, my store!"

Heather ran to the curb and glanced up and down the street.

"What are you doing?" Callum said.

"If someone didn't find what they wanted from my apartment, they'll try my shop next."

"Don't you have a security system?"

"Yes, but that doesn't mean anything, especially in this town." The woman stepped to the curb. "Taxi," Heather yelled as she waved her hand.

One of New York's yellow chariots pulled up, and Heather quickly entered. Callum dove in.

"You must have a death wish."

"Nah, I just like paying for your taxi rides. I have too much money as it is. My accountant said it would be better for my tax position to reduce my ready cash."

"Have you considered suing your accountant for malpractice? Or did you mistake paying for my taxi rides as a capital investment?"

"Where to, lady?" the cabbie asked.

Heather gave him the address for Shop BIO, and the cabbie hit the gas hard, slamming them against the back seat.

"It might be an investment," Callum said. "I'm putting money down that you'll see me as a good guy."

"You'll lose that bet, Special Agent Reilly. You've done everything possible to lose my trust."

Callum reached for her hand, but she pulled it away.

"Don't," Heather said.

The taxi stopped at the high rise that housed the store, and Callum paid before getting out. Heather glared at him as he shut the cab's door.

"Go home, Reilly. You needn't worry about my problems."

"I'm not letting you enter that store alone after someone broke into your apartment."

"You what?" Heather said incredulously.

"You heard me," he said.

Heather rolled her eyes.

"Did you just roll your eyes at me?"

"What? You want to put me over your knee and spank me? Oh, please, sir," she said in a singsong voice. "Don't spank me."

Heather shook her head with a bemused smile on her face that made Callum want to spank her luscious ass, as inappropriate as that thought was. Instead, she strode towards the front door of the building. Callum followed, determined not to let her walk away from him.

When he got close enough to whisper in her ear, he said, "Don't you want me to spank you?"

She snorted in amusement. "No."

She reached the front entrance of Shop BIO, unlocked the door, and flipped the light switch. Fluorescent lights flickered through the store's length, revealing the shop's leather goods and toys on shelves, racks, and under the two long glass counters that ran the right side of the shop.

Callum drew his service weapon. "Lock the door and stay right here."

"What are you doing?"

"Checking for intruders."

She waved her hand dismissively. "Be my guest."

He moved forward cautiously and checked each aisle, catching every footfall of his boots while straining to capture any unusual sound. At the gap between the glass display counters, he pivoted and walked to the black curtain.

"What's this?"

"The backroom where we keep back stock and my workroom."

He peered inside, but it was dark.

"Lights?"

"Right-hand side," Heather said.

He fumbled for the switch and finally turned on the light. More fluorescents flickered overhead, hanging from wood beams. Against the furthest wall were two sewing machines on a wall-to-wall workbench. To the right were several doors, and he opened them, to find in one an empty storeroom and in another a half-bath.

"Satisfied?" She stood with her arms crossed, leaning against the door frame.

"No, I'm not satisfied, Miss Skye."

The smoldering gaze she gave him burned straight to his soul. He looked away, looking at different items in the back room. His eye lit on an X-shaped cross with a leather-covered rail at the bottom, thin leather pillow in the middle, rings at each of the four corners. Though it was freestanding, thick wooden planks ran from the back as feet, connected by a perpendicular plank. For extra strength, another beam ran from the middle of the cross to the furthest rail. It was solid and could bear weight up to five hundred pounds without moving.

"What's that?" he asked impulsively.

"Special order," Heather said.

"You made that?"

"No, I padded and covered the kneeling bench and put in the comfort pillow in the middle."

"That hardly looks comfortable."

"You want to try it? I could use a model."

"No, thanks."

"What?" she said with a wicked glint in her eye. "Afraid?"

"You don't frighten me."

She walked to him with measured, sensuous steps while keeping her eyes trained on him.

"But you should be afraid. I'm not the type of woman to trifle with."

"I'm not trifling."

"Sure. Mr. Big Man with a gun. Put that thing away."

She snapped her words in such a way that it reminded him of his drill sergeant in boot camp.

"I thought we established that doesn't work on me," he said. He met Heather's eyes and didn't pull away, even though it seemed he stared into the orbs of the devil herself.

"Put. The. Gun. Away," she repeated. She reached behind her back and pulled something from it. Her hand snapped, and the leather whip snaked forward and struck the hand in which he held the gun. Pain raced through him with the sudden shock and made him open his hand and drop the weapon.

"What the fuck?" he spat. He bent and picked up the gun and stuck it in his holster. "That's fucking dangerous."

"I'm not the one that got disarmed," she said. "Besides, you had on the safety." She stepped with catlike grace within a pace of Callum. "That hand looks sore."

"Damn right, it's sore." He shook it as a red welt deepened.

"Sorry, but you really must learn your lesson." She took his hand without asking and examined it, and to his surprise, pressed her lips to the welt, then trailed her tongue along the red line she created. Callum stood frozen as delicious sensations of relief shivered through his body, and his cock tingled, then stirred. God, he wanted her, the soft and hard parts of Miss Heather Skye. Just her musky scent short-circuited his brain. He'd do anything to have her.

"Fuck," he said again in a gravelly voice.

She peered up at him with her green eyes filled with danger and sin.

"Pain and pleasure can go hand in hand," she husked.

"Show me," he said. "Show me all of it."

# 16

## HEATHER

Heather sucked in a breath, surprised by Callum's words.

*Show me everything.*

Callum couldn't know what he asked. He barely had dipped his toes in the BDSM world and didn't fathom the depth of *that world*.

"What makes you think you are worthy of *my* attention?" Heather said with a snarl.

Callum blinked, startled at her harsh words.

"What makes you think you'd make a worthy sub? I've trained men half your size who'd begged for what I dished out and relish every moment. I'm not sure *you* could." She curled the leather whip and gripped it in the center, and stuck the end under his chin.

"What are you doing?" he growled.

"Showing you everything."

"Insulting me?"

"Subs, but male subs in particular, love the humiliation and find it a safe place."

"It's sick."

"How will you learn if you dismiss my lessons?"

"I didn't expect—"

"Callum," Heather sighed. "What you don't understand is to live in the moment. Don't *expect*." She turned her back to him and pushed her butt at his hips. She turned her head to glance at him over her shoulder, then reached for and held his chin as she teased him by pressing her butt against him. His Adam's Apple bobbed as he swallowed hard, and his breathing grew shallow as his dick grew hard under her.

"A sub lives at the edge of anticipation. Will my mistress touch me or let me touch her? Can I please my mistress? Because I want to please her very much."

"Is that what submissive men want?"

"It's a part of it."

Heather turned and put her hands on his chest and pushed away.

"Under his mistress' domination, a sub can relax and not fight his anxiety-ridden cultural expectations. The sub needn't be strong, or alpha, or anything else."

"But I'm not anxious."

"Are you not? The first thing you did when you entered my store was to draw your weapon—a phallic symbol."

"I assessed the threat level and provided protection."

Heather cocked an eyebrow. "Or were you displaying your anxiety level at entering a new space where you clearly did not feel safe? A space owned and controlled by a woman. Such anxiety comes from only one place. You learned women were powerless and needed a male to protect them."

"Of course, women need protection."

Heather sighed again. "Our first sense of safety comes from our mothers, who feed and nurture us. But men strip women of their power to make themselves feel powerful."

"That's ridiculous."

"Oh? And how did your father treat your mother?"

His next words came out as an angry growl. "Leave my parents out of this."

Heather smiled. "Thus proving my point."

"This is ridiculous," Callum said. He tried to walk past her, but she refused to budge.

"Move out of my way."

"What are you afraid of, Callum?"

"This is not what I meant."

She pressed the folded whip onto his chest. "You want just the sexy parts? It doesn't work like that, Callum."

He shot a glare at her.

"Insulting and pushing me around works?"

"Haven't you heard anything I said? You wanted me to show you everything. But, to arrive at the sexy parts for which you are eager, you need to understand the power dynamics we're exploring. Otherwise, what happens will leave you confused."

"I don't need you to explain male/female power dynamics."

"Well, tell me, Mr. Alpha Male, when was your last successful relationship?"

One corner of Callum's mouth quirked upward. "I've been busy with work."

"An excuse. All people need touch. It is a biological need, even for alpha males like you. Especially for alpha males. For many, it's their only real human connection. It is the only safe place, albeit within narrow confines, to experience emotion."

"What's your point?"

Heather pressed her hand and against his chest and licked her lips. She watched as his irises grew wide.

"Human interaction balances the power of the two people involved. How you perceive the other and yourself—weaker, stronger, or more rarely, the same—determines where the power flows. You might think the 'stronger' of the two has the power, but that's not true. The 'weaker' partner holds power because they must give consent to the power exchange. Without the sub's permission, their activities are abuse. And in real BDSM, we do not engage in abuse. Instead, the dominant provides a safe place for the submissive to give their power to the Dom or Domme. And to get to that place requires communication and trust."

"You make it sound so pretty," Callum said with a slight sneer.

"It's not. Human emotions and needs are messy, Callum. They aren't logical, and they don't always follow society's dictates. So, Callum, what do you feel right now?"

He looked away. "What are you offering?"

"There, you expressed the desire for me to give my power to you."

"Did I?"

"Yes." She stepped closer to him, and he closed his eyes.

"For you to feel safe, you want me to offer my body to you, so you need not fear rejection. But what will I get?"

"Fantastic sex?" he said.

"How do I know it would be fantastic?"

"Let me show you."

"Do you possess a clue of what turns me on? What places on my body give me shivers when touched? How sensitive are my nipples or the inside of my thighs? How much pressure should you place on my clit to make me moan? Do I like oral sex? Anal sex? Do you know any of those things?"

"I don't," Callum admitted. "But I'd like to find out."

"Sure, but how much fun would it be for me? Doms and Dommes don't just impose their will. They listen to the sub, find out their fantasies, and provide them. Are you willing to listen to my fantasies?"

"Sure," Callum said.

Heather spun on her heels, walked away from him, then looked at him over her shoulder.

"I want a man to kneel at my feet."

He cocked his head, then nodded, and sunk to his knees, and looked up at her.

"Like this?"

"Not like that. Eyes on the floor," Heather said harshly.

He cast his gaze to the floor.

"But you will need a safe word. Since you are a traditional man, we'll go with traditional. Use the word 'red' when you want to stop what we're doing. Do you understand?"

"Yes, Mistress."

"Wait," she said. "And don't look up."

She walked into the shop and walked to the riding crops and chose one, but as she reentered the backroom, she found him watching her. She cracked the crop on her hand to make a loud slapping noise.

"You are rebellious. I told you what to do."

"Sorry," Callum said.

"Sorry, what? How do you address me?"

He shrugged his shoulders. "How do I?"

"You call me Mistress or Mistress Heather."

"Sorry, Mistress."

He could barely spit the word out, and she sighed. This exercise defied his natural inclinations.

"Not suitable. Not suitable at all." She strode to the middle of the floor and walked around him. She noticed he bunched all his muscles, coiled to attack at the first threat.

This would not work.

"Hold out your hand."

"Didn't we do this once already? Where you show me you wouldn't hurt me?"

"I'm glad you remember. But did I tell you to speak?"

"No, Mistress." He stumbled over the word "mistress" once more.

She gazed at him without hope. She was right about him, and now she had to bring the lesson home.

"Go kneel at the cross and wrap your arms around it."

He cast a doubtful glance at her, but did what she told him. Kneeling and with his arms wrapped around the cross, he was in a vulnerable position, and he drew his muscles tighter than ever. She couldn't go on. Her trained eye detected that he experienced distress, and it would get worse if she continued.

Instead, she strode to the opposite side of the cross and knelt to meet him face to face.

"Look at me," she said.

He opened his eyes.

"You aren't enjoying this, are you?"

"No," he said.

"What happened to you when you were in the service?"

"Who said anything did?"

"Your body. The idea of a physical threat sends your body into a panic."

"No, it doesn't."

"Society and the military trained you to ignore it. And that's a problem. No wonder you haven't had a relationship. Every person who comes into your orbit is a death threat."

"I swear it's not true."

"Callum, I've been a Domme for eight years. I know when someone wants to be touched and when they don't. Tell me what happened."

He shook his head. "I've already discussed it with the VA shrinks."

"No, Callum. You didn't. Someone pulled out a shadow from you of the event that gives you nightmares, and you've been deep in your denial ever since."

"It's none of your fucking business," he snarled.

Heather hung her head and sighed. "Red," she said.

He jerked his head up.

"Red? What do you mean?"

"I'm safe wording out, Callum. I'm stopping this scene. You aren't willing to be honest with me. You can get up now."

Heather scooted out from under the cross, only to face Callum, as he stood before her.

"You have it all wrong," he said.

She shook her head. "I don't think so." She stepped around him, but he caught her arm.

"I want to touch you in the worst way, Heather. Oh, hell."

He pulled her closer and captured her lips with his, and the contract sent shivers down her spine and circled in her lower belly. He tasted as good as a cake with buttercream frosting and was just as forbidden. She should not be kissing this man at all. It was wrong for both of them.

But when he cupped her ass in his hands and pulled her closer, her heart flipped, and she forgot all about what she should and shouldn't do. His tongue pressed against her mouth, and she opened, and their tongues tangled. Callum broke the kiss and then licked behind her ear, and a whimper rose in her throat. He grabbed the back of her neck as he scattered kisses on her neck and the swell of her breasts barely held in by her corset. Her head spun from the sheer pleasure of his lips on her flesh. He lifted her from her butt, and she wrapped her legs around his waist. But he whirled to press her back against the cross. Then he yanked the corset's zipper tab, so her breasts spilled out. He sucked her dusky nipples and licked and nibbled on them, and her mouth went dry. All she could think of was getting him inside her.

She squirmed wantonly against him.

"Okay, okay," he said breathlessly. He slapped a leg, and she lowered them from his hips. He stared at her with smoldering eyes as he unbuttoned his pants and let them drop. His cock strained against the fabric of his cotton underwear, and she stared at it. She licked her lips.

"How do you get those leather pants off?" he said in a husky voice.

"The laces at the back."

"Turn," he said. And she felt his hands tugging at the leather laces.

## 17

### CALLUM

Callum stared at Heather's perfect ass as he pulled at the laces that kept her flesh bound. It was a shame to pull down the supple, black leather that clung to the round globes of her ass, but then it was a shame not to. She gripped the edges of the St. Andrew's Cross as if she'd fall if she didn't.

Her flushed face and ragged breathing told Callum she wanted him. Her knees buckled a bit when he peeled the leather down her creamy legs. He licked his lips, imagining what she tasted like, and he got caught between competing desires. He hadn't ever wanted a woman this much, and she was right about one thing. He had a lot to learn about her, and he wanted it all.

His cock stood rock hard and throbbing and it couldn't wait, either. But he was a responsible man, so he bent and pulled a condom from his wallet in his pants pocket.

She looked over her shoulder as the foil ripped. He winked at her as he rolled the condom onto his cock. He leaned forward.

"I'm hot for you, you luscious woman. I've got to have you."

"God help me, Callum, I want you." She spread her legs and pushed her ass out and he lost any reason to wait. Could she be any more perfect?

"You're gorgeous," he breathed. His hand trembled as he guided his cock to her entrance and when he slid inside her channel, she gasped as her channel clenched around him.

"You okay?" he asked. God, she felt so good, he could barely get out the words.

"Better than, baby," she said. Heather wriggled her hips and tossed a smile at him.

"Oh, God," he groaned. He pulled back a bit and sunk inside her again. Her inner walls rippled against him, driving him to take her as deeply as he could. All thoughts centered on her as he plunged inside. She groaned and pushed back against him.

"More!" she said.

He thrust inside her with his thoughts centered on her heat, and luscious scent, and soft skin. His balls tingled and ached, coaxing him to his release. He bit his lip, fighting the rising sensation urging him to let go. Under him, Heather gripped the two sides of the cross, her body tensed, and then she cried out in a long, joyful cry. Her walls gripped him, and he couldn't hold on any longer. He clasped her hips and pummeled her with wild abandon. She cried out again in another orgasm, and this last one was too much. He spilled inside the condom as he exploded.

He wrapped his arms around her waist and laid his head on her back as his ragged breathing slowed. An unaccustomed warmth spread through his chest and he kissed her back.

Heather squirmed under him and pulled away enough so she could turn. But when she did, he put his hands on either side of the cross and kissed her. This kiss was long, slow, and filled with passion.

She sighed when he pulled away.

"You are amazing," he said with a wide smile.

"You are, too."

"Let's take this someplace more comfortable," he suggested.

She sucked on her lip, looking unsure. This was the first time he'd ever seen that expression on her face.

"I should get home."

He shook his head. "Nope. Because of that break-in, not unless I go with you, though technically it is my apartment, now. I sent Aaron the rent for the next two months today."

"And what am I supposed to do for an apartment? My new one isn't ready yet."

He raised his eyebrows. "You can always share with me until you move out."

"Moving a little fast, aren't you there, cowboy?"

It didn't occur to him, but now that she mentioned it, he could see why she would think like that. But that's not what he meant. He could always sleep on the couch if need be, and it was only to protect her. But he didn't need to stay at Aaron's apartment. He still had time left on the monthly rental of his hotel room.

He was about to tell her all that when scratching at the back door caused both of them to stare in that direction.

"You expecting anyone?" Callum said.

"Not at this time of night," Heather said.

"Get dressed," he said.

"You don't have to tell me twice." She shrugged into her leather pants and clipped the metal closures on her corset together while the scratching grew louder.

Callum slipped off the condom and tied it off before he dropped it in a wastebasket, and pulled on his pants. Then he toed his ankle-high boots on while he pulled out his phone from his pocket.

"I want you to get out of here and go to my hotel." He tried to hand her his keycard, but she shook her head.

"If you think I'm leaving you alone in my shop, you're nuts. Plus, that door is supposed to be 100% impenetrable."

"Nothing is, and it sounds like someone is using a tire iron to pry open the door. Go, Heather."

"A store owner goes down with the store." Heather's expression hardened with determination. She snatched her whip, and Callum admitted she could wield it like a deadly weapon. But her leather was no match for a gun if the intruder possessed one.

He pulled his weapon from its holster and pointed it at the back door. Heather stepped to the wall and flicked off the light.

The back door broke open with a loud crack, and Callum pointed his gun toward it. A streetlight backlit a shadowy figure. Heather flicked the light on, blinding Callum, but also the intruder.

"Oh, snap," a youngish voice said.

"It's just a kid," Heather said with surprise.

Callum's eyesight cleared to find a skinny red-headed teen standing frozen in the doorway. The kid's eyes widened with fear.

"Get on the floor, hands on your head." Callum held his gun forward and trained on the intruder.

"Who the fuck are you?" the teen said.

"NYPD, asshole. What the hell were you thinking, breaking into this store?"

"Well, you can't see anything from the outside windows, and I got curious."

"On your knees, now," Callum ordered.

"Hmmm," Heather said in a low voice. "A girl could get used to orders spoken like that."

Callum's mouth twitched in a half-smile. "Nice to know." He turned his attention to the intruder. "Kid, I swear to God, since Fallujah, I shoot first and ask questions later. On your knees, or Miss Heather here will whip your ass. And she's pretty good with leather whips."

The kid glanced from Callum's face to the gun, then to Heather, standing there with the expression of an avenging angel, and fell to his knees.

Callum returned his gun to its holster and pulled out his handcuffs and snapped them on the kid's wrists. "I hope you're curious to see the inside of a jail cell."

"Callum, must you?" Heather said. "He's just a kid."

"I watched a crime in progress. Yes."

"Your girlfriend? She hot."

Callum frowned. He didn't want to sort out his relationship with Heather at this moment. Sure, they'd just had sex, but he realized he didn't know how she felt about that. Plus, she stood there with her hands on her hips with a disapproving expression on her face. His face flushed. Why did that angry look turn him on? Callum shook his head. He had to keep his mind on the job.

"Shut up, asshole. What's your name?"

"Figure it out for yourself."

"Don't want Mommy to know what you are doing out of bed, eh?"

Callum whipped out his phone and speed-dialed dispatch. "This is Detective Callum Reilly." He rattled out his badge number and requested pickup for breaking-and-enter suspect.

"And the address, Detective?"

Callum looked toward Heather. "What's the address?"

Heather opened her mouth, and then her eyes widened.

"Put the phone down, cop. And let the kid go."

Callum turned to find a .45 pointed at him. He stared at a large dark-haired man who glared at him.

The lights went out, leaving them in the dark. Like before, the streetlight backlit the person in the doorway, only this time the person was larger and holding a pistol.

Callum took the momentary distraction to rush the intruder

and pushed him back with a tackle. They both fell against the concrete block retaining wall and the man grunted.

"Jesus Christ," the intruder huffed. "Give me a hand."

From the corner of his eye, Callum caught the movement of two men rushing toward them. One set of hands pulled him off the dark-haired intruder, while another held him fast. The large man stood, shook himself off, then he took two steps forward and punched Callum in the gut. Callum held in a grunt as a wave of pain spread through him.

"Hey," Heather said. "Leave him alone."

"Mind your business, missy. This has nothing to do with you."

"Heather," Callum said. "Go back inside. I'll handle this."

"Get him to the car."

"What about the girl?" The voice wheezed as if he'd smoked too many cigarettes in his life.

"Can't touch her. She's protected."

Callum struggled to get free, but these guys had him locked in firmly between them.

The crack of a whip reverberated through the alleyway.

"I said leave him alone," Heather said with deadly determination.

"Lady, get back inside that pretty little store of yours before I shoot it and you up, protected or not. And stay away from the cops. They aren't good for your health. Come on, kid. Get off that floor and let's go. And you, lady? You haven't seen us, and you didn't know where the cop went. Got that?"

"Don't you dare hurt him," Heather said.

The big man scoffed. "Shut that door now, and I'll forget that you mouthed off to me."

"Callum," Heather shouted.

"Do as he says," Callum called out. "I don't need your help."

"Callum, I won't—" Heather said.

"There's not a damn thing you can do. Get inside, Heather," Callum snarled. "Don't go risking anything for me. You weren't as good of a fuck as you think. So there's no need to place yourself in danger, Miss Protected Person." The last words he spoke with all the venom he could muster.

Heather's eyes flew opened wide and then narrowed.

He closed his eyes as she slammed the door shut.

"Put him in the fucking trunk," the big man said. "I don't want to hear a word from him on the way there."

## 18

"How dare he! Miss Protected Person, indeed!" she sputtered. Why the hell would he speak those words to her? "What an ass!" He said those words, sounding as if he didn't care after they had made love. Or maybe it wasn't love. Their passion was hot and sweaty, and maybe not love, but in her heart, it was the closest thing to feeling affection for someone other than Kristal she had experienced for a long time.

As she slammed the metal door, Heather shook with the force of anger blazing through her body. She felt hurt by his words but also frightened. Watching Callum getting hauled away by those gangsters rocked her to her soul. She had faced many things in her life, but she never dealt with gangsters. Like any streetwise gal, she knew they were bad news and avoided them.

She still didn't believe Callum that Master William was knee-deep with organized crime. She had known the Dom for nearly a decade and saw nothing, except for the past few days, that suggested that he even knew Mafia-connected people.

She pushed the door open and stared at the ruined lock. That kid must have wanted to get inside the shop badly because he'd pried not only the lock but bent the door jamb. It would cost hundreds of dollars to fix it. The kid did a thorough, even professional job of prying open the entryway, and she had to get this fixed. And that grated on her because she was more worried about Callum than the damned store entrance.

God, she hated having to focus on this instead of his plight. The store housed hundreds of thousands of dollars in merchandise, and she couldn't ignore that, or her responsibility to her partner. Kristal warned her often about going to the store late at night.

She pulled out her phone and started searching for all-night locksmiths. She called a couple until she got an answer from a sleepy-sounding guy who said he'd be right out. With one problem on the way to getting solved, she called Kristal.

"Hey."

"Hey?" Kristal said.

"Someone broke into the shop and destroyed the back door."

"What!" Kristal said in alarm.

"Relax. I'm here. The store is safe."

"What? Are you okay? What are you doing at the shop at this hour? And how can you talk to me so coolly when you faced a robber?"

"It was a kid, looking for thrills."

"Still—"

"Don't worry about me," Heather insisted. "I'll make sure the door is secure. But this may stretch on for hours, so please open the store in the morning."

"Are you sure I can't help? Bring coffee? Moral support? God, Heather. You must be freaked."

"I'm fine," Heather stubbornly insisted. "It's Callum—"

"Callum? The 'I-wouldn't-be-caught-dead-with-him' Callum?"

"Hush. This is serious. Three thugs hauled him off."

"In front of you? And you're not out of your mind about that —how?"

Heather huffed. "What do you expect me to do, Kristal? Callum insisted he go with them."

"He did?"

"I couldn't stop him, even when I tried."

"You what?" Heather could imagine Kristal's wide-open mouth. Her best friend's next words were utterly Kristal.

"And these gangsters had guns?"

"Well..." hedged Heather.

"Heather Skye, how dare you put yourself in danger? If you let yourself get hurt, I'll kill you."

Heather scoffed. "Don't worry about me, Mrs. Stirling. I have always taken care of myself."

"Wow, show a gal a little love, and this is what I get. Look, I'm coming there."

"No, don't—"

But the phone clicked off before Heather could get those words out.

"Fabulous," she muttered. Now she'd have to deal with a locksmith in the middle of the night and her best friend hovering over her.

She didn't understand what Kristal was worried about. The woman had experienced Heather's inner nature stoic nature during a crisis. And Kristal had also witnessed that after the crisis passed, Heather would become a blubbering mess.

As Heather stood in the chilly New York night, police lights flickered at the end of the alleyway. She huffed. Callum had called in the kid's arrest, and now they were here to pick up the teen.

Two uniformed officers approached her, both holding their hands over their holsters. These guys were ready for conflict.

"Dispatch sent us to assist Detective Reilly," one said.

Heather turned toward them and put her hands on her hips. "It's about time you showed up. Not only did a thug pry open my security door, but three gangsters hauled off Detective Reilly."

The two officers glanced at each other.

"Say again?" one officer said.

"Three thugs dragged Detective Reilly away. I don't know who the men were, or why they did."

Both police officers stared at her with suspicion in their eyes, as if silently accusing her of being part of the plot. Heather didn't blame them because she should be sharing Callum's fate just for witnessing the criminals' crimes. The crack about being protected nagged her. Who was protecting her, and why? She resisted the urge to bite her lip.

One officer turned away and spoke into the radio at his shoulder while the other glared at her as if she were the source of all his troubles.

"What happened?" he said.

"Detective Reilly and I, well, never mind about that. But we heard noises at the back of my business, and the door flew open. This kid pried off the lock. Detective Reilly was about to put handcuffs on him when the gangsters arrived and took him."

"And do you have a reason they didn't take you, too?"

Heather shook her head as her mouth went dry. No way she'd admit to hearing the "she's protected" remark. That would open a line of inquiry she did not want to face. And one she would need to ask Master William about—if she could find him.

"We need you to come to Chi-town precinct and give your statement."

"I need to wait until my partner gets here. In this town, an open door is an invitation to 'bye-bye merchandise.'"

"And that's what you worry about? Not a police officer's life?" said the officer with a hard edge in his voice.

No. That wasn't the only thing she worried about, but

Callum seemed determined to go with the gangsters. Damn it, why did Callum have the power to confuse her and toss her life into disarray?

"Just a minute," said a deeper voice.

The two officers glanced backward, and Heather followed their eyes. A man dressed in a leather jacket, white tee-shirt, and dark pants approached them. A police badge clipped to his belt peeked out from under his open jacket.

"Captain," greeted one officer.

"Suarez, Epson. What do we know?"

"Not much. Our one witness refuses to give any useful information." One officer pointed his finger at Heather.

Heather snorted. The officer was trying to goad her, probably to induce her to spill her guts. Well, she'd keep her guts.

The corner of the captain's mouth twitched, the only tell in an otherwise professional neutral expression. "Okay. I've got this. Go canvass the area. See if there were any witnesses to these men taking our detective."

"Yes, sir."

In the poorly lit alley, the police captain strode toward Heather. It wasn't until he grew closer that she saw he was in his forties, with graying hair at his temples.

"I'm Captain Watrous. I'm Detective Reilly's superior officer."

"His boss," she said in a flat voice.

"You could say that."

"Only he had more than one boss," Heather said. "And I suppose that one takes precedence."

Watrous raised an eyebrow in surprise. "He told you about that?"

Heather snorted in derision. "There's little that men don't tell me, Captain."

"So you know that he needs to wrap up his investigation in a month before he leaves town?"

Heather pursed her lips and looked away. A month? He'd be gone in a month? Why the hell didn't he say something? Why had he been trying so hard to get her to pay attention to him? Her eyes narrowed. It must be all part of Callum's plot to get "in" with William Ianucci. She huffed. She should have known that Callum was just using her.

"Of course," Heather said.

"That wouldn't stop our investigation of the Ianuccis though," the captain said. "I would just assign someone else."

Heather crossed her arms and glared at the captain.

"And I kept telling Callum, and I'm telling you now. There is nothing to find on William Ianucci. He's a business owner and not a crime boss. You need to look elsewhere."

Watrous shook his head. "Detective Reilly is sharp. I trust his instincts."

"Fine, trust what you want."

"Heather? You okay?"

At the end of the alley stood Kristal and Aaron. How could they get here so quickly? And then it hit Heather that Kristal and Aaron's new apartment stood only three blocks from the store. A cab would get them here almost instantly at this time of night. God, she must be more rattled than she thought.

"I'm fine, Kristal. Come meet my new friend. Captain Watrous, NYPD, Chi-Town Precinct."

Consummate salesman Aaron strode to the captain and held out his hand.

"Thank you for your service, Captain. Though you are off your beat, aren't you?"

"I go where I need to. And you are?"

"Aaron Stirling. My wife, Kristal, is Heather's business partner. My business is in this building, too. JLG Advertising."

"Good, then I can take Miss Skye to the precinct while you deal with the problem here."

"Are you arresting Heather?"

"I should say not," erupted Heather. "I did nothing wrong."

"You are a material witness to a police officer's kidnapping. The law says I can hold you."

"Good," Aaron said.

"Good?" Heather said angrily.

"Being a material witness means he doesn't believe you committed a crime," Aaron said confidently.

"Yeah, until the police decide I did. No way am I going with you, Watrous, without an arrest warrant."

"In these circumstances, I don't need one."

"I'm calling our lawyer," Kristal said.

"You do that, miss. In the meantime, Miss Skye, come along with me. Don't make me handcuff you."

## 19

After fifteen minutes of stop-and-go driving, which tossed Callum forward and back in the car trunk, the vehicle sped up. The muffled sounds of the car's radio playing and the tha-dump, tha-dump, tha-dump from the vehicle rolling over the seams and potholes of a New York concrete highway filled the small compartment.

He was used to potholes from riding in MSFVs, Mobile Strike Force Vehicles, and Humvees in Afghanistan. The war vehicles' solid construction protected you, but they were built for war, not comfort. A hard jolt sent your head into the vehicle's ceiling. Though it was now after midnight, it was stifling hot and stuffy inside the trunk of this car. It made his head swim, but he'd hang in there. He'd been through worse.

Wherever the thugs were taking him, whoever he'd face, he could handle it. War, fighting, facing the enemy—these were things he understood well.

What he did not, or rather, who he did not understand, was Miss Heather Skye. One minute she was hard as nails, and the next, she was as gentle as a kitten. She was a puzzle wrapped in a leather corset and thigh-high leather boots. The woman was pure sex, and he licked his lips at the thought of tasting her mouth once more.

His right hand, which had caught the tips of her whip, swelled and ached. Yeah, she was a kitten with sharp claws, but he liked the way he made her purr. He took a deep breath when he thought about being inside her. If he weren't so uncomfortable, he would have to take a hand to his cock to seek relief, but he could barely move. One foot had fallen asleep, and the slight wiggles he could manage with his toes did nothing to relieve the pins and needles sensation in his feet. He'd regret being so eager to climb into the gangster's trunk just to find out what the hell was going on.

Though he should be afraid, these guys running around wearing slacks and polo shirts and brandishing Glocks didn't ignite fear in him. Guns and out-of-shape thugs he could handle. If it weren't for Heather standing too close to the action, he would have taken out the three that ambushed him. But he didn't want to risk Heather getting hurt, and he wanted to find out who was behind their organization.

Still, the trip seemed to last an inordinate amount of time, and Callum wondered if they were taking him to New York farmland to dump him in a forsaken location.

*Sure, you survived a half-dozen deployments in different hot spots, including Afghanistan, but New York in your own country was the place that will do you in.*

He shook off this uncomfortable thought. He wasn't a quitter and wouldn't abandon his mission. Hell, his commanding officer wanted him to quit, but he wouldn't do it. He was inches from attaining his aims—if he didn't get killed first.

The car slowed and turned, stopped, and turned again. They must have gotten off at an exit. Callum listened intently to pick up any clue where they were, but heard nothing remarkable.

With another turn, the car's wheels crunched gravel, and the ride got bumpier. The sound of gravel meant they weren't going off-road, giving him hope they didn't plan to put a bullet in his head and toss his lifeless body somewhere.

The car stopped, throwing him against the trunk latch.

"Sonofabitch."

The trunk opened, but someone shone a light in his eyes so he couldn't see.

"Put this on."

Fabric fell onto his hands. It seemed to be a hood. That sucked because it would make it more difficult to get his bearings. But it was good, because if they were trying to hide information from him, they didn't have plans to kill him—at least not yet.

"Hurry," growled one in a nasty tone.

Callum put the hood over his head, and two men hauled him roughly from the truck. He stumbled on his nerve-numbed feet, and one of his handlers jerked him upright.

"What's wrong with you? Move it."

"Give me a freaking chance. You had me folded up in that trunk, and my feet fell asleep."

"Just get him up there," said the deeper voice. He recognized this as the voice of the portly man that held the gun on him and Heather. Yeah, he'd like a crack at that guy. He deserved an attitude adjustment. But blindfolded, with a gangster on either side clasping his arms, he was in no position to give anyone a lesson.

They half-yanked, half-dragged him up on a pathway.

"Steps," one said in a grating voice. Callum did his best to navigate the stairs under his feet, but his escorts had no particular care for his comfort and jerked him up one stair after another.

"Open the door," said one, and the man at his right let go of his arm.

"Inside," his handler said.

Callum stepped forward, and a door slammed behind him. The scent of lemon oil and old varnish hit his nose.

"Take him into the library. The boss is waiting."

"Sure, let's go, cop," growled the man that held him.

Another door creaked opened and the aromatic scent of cigar smoke greeted Callum's nose. The heavy scent, nuanced with dark chocolate, wood, and spices, reminded him of the baby shower he attended at Sean Cashman's. Wherever he was, it wasn't a backroom meant for rough business.

"Sit," growled his handler as he steered Callum to it.

"You mind?" Callum said. He pointed to his hood.

*"Per l'amor del cielo, stunad."*

"Sorry, boss. Take it off, cop."

"Go," the boss growled in a thin, gravely voice.

Callum blinked as he removed the hood, and waited until his eyes adjusted to find Gabriel Russo staring at him from behind a massive wood desk. He steepled his hands as he looked over Callum as if assessing him.

Gabriel Russo looked every bit of a wizened eighty-something old man. Against the backdrop of shelves of ancient books and the massive oak desk, he appeared dwarfed by his surroundings. But Callum had little doubt that the man wasn't as defenseless as he appeared. He probably had a gun within reach somewhere in that desk.

"Please forgive my associates. They misunderstood my intentions."

"So you're saying that you didn't intend to kidnap me?"

The elderly man chuckled.

"I needed you away from the prying eyes of the NYPD. They've had me under surveillance for the longest time."

"You mean the FBI. Because the police don't spend those type of resources for long-term surveillance."

"On that you'd be wrong, Detective."

A door opened on the left, and Callum's head turned to see William Ianucci step into the library.

"Is your wife okay?" Russo said.

Ianucci frowned. "She's not happy with me, but Samantha's glad I'm okay, especially after Detective Reilly's visit to our apartment." Ianucci met Callum's eyes with a hard stare.

"I knew you were NYPD. But the NCIS thing is something else."

Russo raised his eyebrows, but said nothing.

"Your wife told you why I visited?"

"She did. We hide nothing from each other. And you frightened her badly, which I do not appreciate."

"I'm just doing my job, Ianucci."

"Which doesn't include scaring people not involved in this."

"Gil," Russo said, "let's put that aside for now, and get to business."

Callum's mouth twitched. "Yes, let's get down to it."

Russo scoffed. "And you can put your attitude away, Detective Reilly. We intend to help you."

Now it was Callum's time to scoff. He didn't trust what either of these two had to say. "Why?"

Russo spat to one side.

"Because," he snarled, "we are not traitors to this country."

"But all accounts, you are both criminals," Callum said. "What's a little treason to you?"

"You are an arrogant bastard," spat Russo. "My family and Gil's family came here with nothing. You think it was easy to survive in a new country, with fine Americans insulting us with vile names, and not being able to get work? Look at you! I'll bet your family came over on the *Mayflower*."

"You don't need to tell me about discrimination against immigrants. My family came from Ireland. They weren't welcome either."

"Yeah, we also know the corruption the Irish brought to the city's politics here."

"Uncle Gitchy, that's old history and not helping us here," Ianucci said.

"You're right, Gil. You've always been smart. Tell him, before I crack his skull."

Ianucci crossed his arms and walked across the room.

"We've been watching you, Reilly, since you showed up here a year ago. We didn't know why you took an interest in the club, or me, or even Miss Heather."

"This has nothing to do with Heather."

"I wouldn't want to be you when you face her next. She will not appreciate being used."

"I didn't—"

"Save your explanations for her. I don't care about your excuses. What I care about is my business and my family, and I don't want any of that torn apart by a bull-in-a-china-shop detective. You hung around and did your best to get in with us, and I didn't understand it. Then Gitchy—Gabriel—came to me about what he heard about certain people doing things they shouldn't. Gabriel looked into it for me with certain contacts he had. That's when I pieced together your interest in me. You think I'm laundering money for a terrorist organization."

"Aren't you?"

William scoffed. "It didn't occur to you I love my country even if my family wasn't always on the up-and-up, did it? That we appreciated the opportunity to put down roots and build a life? That betraying our country is not in our DNA?"

"Because organized crime is such a wholesome thing."

"Watch your mouth," Russo said. "Gil here has done his best to put his family on the right side of the law. He couldn't help what his family did, but he made it right for them. And now there is a punk like you sniffing around looking to make trouble for him. I won't have it."

"Uncle Gitchy, I can fight my own fights."

"Sure you can, Gil. I just want Detective Reilly to know our patience is limited."

"And so is mine," Callum said. "What do you want from me?"

Ianucci's mouth formed a hard line.

"I want you to leave my family and business alone."

Ianucci's expression confirmed he sincerely wanted that. Did that mean Ianucci was ready to strike a deal? There was only one way to find out.

"And what do I get for that?"

"In the old days—" growled Russo.

"Uncle Gitchy, we'll handle this my way."

"He better do his job, or it's my neck and yours on the line."

"You don't need to tell me the stakes, Uncle Gitchy. But what they are doing is not right, and this is the best way to handle it. Besides, you can always go visit my parents in Florida."

Russo scoffed. "Not happening."

Ianucci shrugged and leveled his gaze at Callum.

"Uncle Gitchy checked around for my sake, and it raised the suspicions of the people you are looking for. That's why he's hiding out here until you do your job. We're ready to give you the names of the people who are laundering money for this Red Talon organization, and where you can find the evidence. But if you screw this up, we're all dead."

## 20

Heather didn't embarrass easily, so she could only attribute the burning in her cheeks to sheer agitation as she waited in Watrous' office in the Chi-town police precinct. She disliked this police station and the bustle of activity swirling in the detective's room, and the outwardly hostile glances of different detectives as they glanced into their captain's office. Callum's kidnapping stirred a hornet's nest of police activity, as all hands reported in response to the crisis. The somber mood in the precinct made a funeral a joyful event by comparison, and the fact Captain Watrous insisted she hang out in his office grated on her nerves.

The only good thing about this situation was that Jaime Wilder, her partner's lawyer and now hers, sat next to her, sipping coffee and lending a calming presence in this insane day.

Watrous entered the office once more and settled behind his desk. Another officer, wearing his badge from a chain around his neck, filled the doorway.

"Miss Skye, Attorney Wilder, Detective Matheson. He partners with Callum on certain cases."

"Nice to meet you, Detective," Wilder said.

"Can't say the same. Where is Detective Reilly?"

"My client has no information on Detective Reilly's location. She is, in fact, a crime victim."

"She can answer for herself," said Matheson. "Or can she? She seems as if she doesn't have a brain in her head."

A flash of anger blazed through Heather, and she pivoted in her seat toward the nasty detective, but Wilder laid his hand on her arm.

"He's just goading you, Heather," he said in a low voice.

Heather huffed and faced forward again.

"Believe whatever keeps you warm at night," she said. "I know nothing about the men who attacked us."

"But one of them had the description of Jimmy Mack."

"If you call size a resemblance, but no, it wasn't Jimmy Mack."

Matheson pounced on that piece of information with the intensity of a cat hunting a mouse.

"So you know Jimmy Mack?" His question hung in the air filled with expectation.

Heather huffed and then frowned.

"I met him precisely once."

"And that was when?"

"I don't see the point of your question. I meet many people because I own a store and frequent a popular BDSM club."

"Are you saying Jimmy Mack goes to *La Corda Rosa*?" Captain Watrous said.

"No." Heather crossed her arms and stared at the captain.

"Is there a point to asking these questions yet again?" Wilder said. "It's getting late, and my client is exhausted."

"Listen, you shyster—" Matheson said.

"Fine, if you refuse to be cordial, I'm taking my client home. Heather?" Wilder got to his feet.

Watrous cleared his throat. "Matheson, check with Sergeant Sloan about any calls with info from other precincts."

"But Captain–"

"Go, Matheson."

Matheson shot a parting glare at Heather and Wilder before exiting, and then Heather heard, "What the fuck—?"

"Nice to see you too, Matheson. Hey, Captain, why is everyone here?"

Heather turned her head to spot Callum in the doorway.

"Half the precinct has been searching for you," said Matheson, who now stood behind Callum.

"A sec," Callum said. "I need—"

Callum's eyes lit on Heather. "What are you—"

Heather huffed once more, this time with immense irritation. "There's your boy, all safe and sound, Captain Watrous. Goodbye." She rose and walked to exit the detective's room with Wilder behind her.

Callum edged around her to meet her face to face. He nodded towards Jaime. "Who's that guy?" Callum said. He eyed Wilder with suspicion.

"He's my lawyer, one the NYPD forced me to hire because your captain proclaimed I was some sort of material witness. Now, if you'll excuse me, I'm cranky and tired—a dangerous combination."

"Wait, Heather. I must speak with you."

"After what you put me through? After you lied to me? Used me to worm your way closer to your 'suspects' in your investigation? Drew criminals to my store? It will be a hot summer's day in the middle of a winter before I speak with you again. Excuse me."

Heather struggled to keep her fury in check and had to escape from the police station and Callum before she did something that would land her in jail.

Callum stepped aside, and she strode past him.

"Reilly, in here," Watrous said.

Callum held up a finger begging for a minute, and turned an earnest gaze to Heather.

"Heather, please wait. I can explain everything."

Heather shot him a frosty glance. "Of course you can, but I won't believe you. Let's go, Jaime. Maybe you can buy a girl a drink?"

Her stiletto heels clicked on the worn hardwood floor as she strode from the detectives' room. Imagine Reilly thinking he could explain things away as if she were a teenage girl angry with her boyfriend. He was entirely lucky to be standing in a police station because her first inclination was to bend him over her knee and give him a good thrashing. She couldn't do that, because it was inappropriate, but it was a thought.

Outside the precinct house, Heather glanced at Wilder.

"Go home," she said.

"No, I'll escort you to your apartment."

She shook her head. "I'm a big girl. I can handle getting to my apartment."

"Sure you can, but didn't you tell me someone broke into your apartment? You shouldn't go there alone."

"Jaime, I'll be fine. Thanks for everything."

He smiled. "No thanks necessary. You'll get my bill."

"Spoken like a lawyer."

"I'll phone tomorrow to check on you."

"Wow, and customer service, too. Why hasn't some girl snatched you up?"

He laughed. "Oh, they tried. I'm holding out for Ms. Perfect."

She chuckled. "Says every man, everywhere."

Heather thought she caught the lawyer blush, but it was dark, and he wasn't standing under a streetlight. It just might be a trick of the street's ambient illumination.

"Here, let me wave down a cab for you," he said.

She resisted the urge to roll her eyes. Most New Yorkers avoided the cabs and walked instead. But it was late and her apartment seven miles away, and she had no desire to ride a subway home.

"Thanks."

"If Reilly contacts you again, contact me. If they keep after you, we might sue for harassment."

Heather sucked on her lip. "That's unnecessary, Jaime. I don't want the hassle. I'd rather put my energies into my work and my business."

"Still, tell me if Reilly contacts you."

A cab pulled to the curb, and Jaime opened the door for her.

"Such a gentleman," she said with a wink. "Talk to you, tomorrow."

"Goodnight, Heather."

She climbed into the cab, and for the first time all day, Heather could relax. After giving the cabbie her address, she tried to relax. But the seat was hard, and the cabbie barely had the air conditioning cranked. She fanned her face and wished the ride would end soon.

This time of night, the ride wasn't as crazy as a daytime stop-n-go cab adventure, so she didn't stress about the driving. Instead, she mulled over the day's event, and got angry at herself for being so stupid as to fall for Callum's lies. She even made love to him, which now made her sick to her stomach. She despised sneaks and liars, and Callum was both. Her hands curled at her sides at the thought, and she banged both fists into her seat.

*He better not cross my path again*, she thought. *He'd find out just how experienced with a whip I am.*

New York City at night was a different animal than in the day. The neon lights, lighting in storefronts, and street lights, gave the dark city street a fairy glow. At night, the city was enlivened kinetically in a way it was not during the mundane day. Even the passing screech of a police car seemed magical.

Heather sucked in a breath, then let it out, to find a hitch in her breathing. She was self-aware enough to know why. She had let Callum into her heart, and he hurt her. Now she must exorcise him from it for her own good.

*I was a fool to trust him.*

It would not be easy. She saw now what took hold inside her was more tenacious than she had realized. Tomorrow she'd down a pint of ice cream, Kristal's recipe for heartache, and maybe get a mani-pedi. Kristal would understand and handle the store on her own. Heather had done it enough times for Kristal. It was her turn now.

*My friend, you should take your vacay time when you aren't nursing a breaking heart. It's more fun that way.*

The cab halted at her apartment. After paying, she left the cab and looked up to her window. It was dark there, as she had expected. Why did she think she'd find a light on?

*You're tired of living alone. After living with Kristal so many years, you don't like coming home to a cold dark apartment. There is no one to share a pizza with, or a joke, or the frustrations of the day.*

She shook her head. She didn't begrudge Kristal finding her forever love, or her friend's marriage. But things weren't the same since Kristal left to live with Aaron. And Heather found she disliked living alone.

*Buck up, Skye. You know there isn't a man for you. You are too different. You need things that most men don't want to give you. And subs, by-and-large, are too focused on their kinky needs to care about yours, and that does not hold your interest. Callum was interesting until he proved to be a rat liar.*

*You're being silly, Heather Skye. All this time you haven't needed a man. Why are you obsessing over a scumbag police officer?*

She pondered this question as she climbed the steps to her apartment.

"Heather!"

She turned to see Callum staring up at her.

"What are you doing here?"

"Well, it is my apartment. I told you that earlier. Remember?"

She scoffed. "I remember whole bunches of things, Detective Reilly."

"We're back to that again," he said with resignation.

"Go home, Detective. The day has been too long and my patience is at an end." She turned and took the steps with quick mincing strides, but that didn't stop the pesky detective. He doggedly followed behind.

She reached the landing for her floor and picked up the pace to make the door. Once behind it, she'd lock it and keep him from bothering her.

But she miscalculated how fast Callum was, and he reached her just as she turned her key in the lock.

She whipped around to face him.

"What do you not understand about 'go home,' and 'leave me alone'?"

Callum shook his head.

"I'll never understand it. I want you, Heather, not just in my bed, but in my life."

"Your bed. Your life. Hah!"

She pushed open the door and hoped to get inside and slam the door.

"Heather, I'm sorry. I sincerely am. I know how it looked to you, like I was using you to get to Ianucci. That's not what I meant; I promise."

"Sure, sure," Heather said. Her voice dripped with sarcasm.

"It only looks that way, but that's exactly what you did. How little respect you showed me. I didn't deserve that."

"What do I have to do to show you I'm sincere?"

"Drop to your knees and kiss my feet," she ordered. Heather was sure Callum couldn't bring himself to perform that act of submission. His inner Dom would never allow it. She gazed into his eyes with the coldest, most steely glance she could muster, and he looked away.

Then to her surprise Callum dropped to his knees and bent his lips to her feet and kissed one stilettoed boot, then the other, and planted kisses on each.

"I'm sorry, Mistress Heather," he said. "I was wrong to disrespect you. Please, forgive me, though I don't deserve it."

Heather swallowed hard. How could he do this? How could this strong, dominant man kneel at her feet and beg forgiveness? This act of submission was everything that ticked off every box in her Domme heart. Seeing the top of his head over her boots made her realize she loved him, utterly and forever.

"You're right. You don't deserve my forgiveness. But I'm afraid I'm quite helpless not to grant it to you."

Callum looked up at her with hope in his eyes, and her heart melted even more.

"Oh, get up," she said. "And get into that apartment. You have penance ahead of you."

## 21

Callum stood and stared into Heather's gorgeous green eyes, which held a seductive twinkle.

"Penance?" Callum flashed her a smile. "What sort of penance?"

She spoke in a low, seductive voice. "The one where I am well satisfied with your services."

Her sexy tone of voice shot sparks straight to his throbbing cock. His pulse quickened as his fingers yearned to touch her skin, and his mouth begged to taste her in her most intimate place. As his breath caught in his chest, he slid his hand on her leather-covered ass and kissed her neck. Her perfume made his head swim. He couldn't resist her and didn't want to.

"Take me to your dungeon," he whispered.

Her eyes sparkled as she pushed the door open with her back. She gathered his shirt in her fist and pulled him inside.

"Bedroom," she ordered.

"Yes, ma'am."

"What did you call me?" She spoke with a deadly edge to her voice.

"Yes, Mistress Heather."

"That's what I like to hear." She smiled wickedly and yanked on his shirt again while walking back slowly into her apartment. He leaned forward to kiss her, but she held her arm rigidly.

"Uh, uh, uh, soldier boy. You don't get a reward yet."

He raised his eyebrows. "No?"

"Nope. You must earn it."

His blood ran like fire through his body and pounded in his ears. "How?"

"Come into my bedroom," she husked. She turned her back to him, then glanced over her shoulder and stared at him so intensely, he swallowed hard. He followed her into the bedroom. With his eyes on her round leather-clad butt, his head wanted to do things to her that a man had no right imagining, like pin her on the bed, and pull down those leather slacks and take her hard. But this was Heather's show, and she wouldn't appreciate him taking over. He'd play it her way, for now.

She pointed to the front of her corset. "Undo the busks."

Callum raised his eyebrows. "Excuse me?"

"The metal closures are called busks."

"Learn a new word every day," he muttered.

"What did you say?" she said sternly.

"Ah, let me try." He stepped in close and pulled at one metal closure with one hand, but the corset stubbornly refused to yield.

"Is this corset painted on?"

"You didn't complain when you stared at my breasts. What... the big man can't handle a few pieces of metal?" Her eyes twinkled with mischief.

"I get your game now. You're teasing me."

She chuckled. "And if I am?"

"Then I know a lady that deserves a spanking."

"You've got that wrong," she said. "I'm not the one that receives spankings."

Callum thought she deserved a stiff paddling, especially for this little game of "busk, busk, who can undo the busk." He attempted once again to release her breasts from the corset. He slipped his fingers under the leather and pulled the two pieces of the corset together to free the first busk.

"Watch it," she said. "The leather doesn't have much give."

Then something stung his finger, and he pulled it away and sucked on it.

"Ouch," Heather said.

"What the hell was that?" Callum said.

She grimaced. "The bra underwire poked through the lining. I told you the leather had no give."

"This is a deadly thing you're wearing."

"You have no idea. Are you going to open up this corset or what?"

"No." He dug into the corset and pulled out the underwire in one good tug.

"Hey!" she protested. "That's a thousand-dollar corset." She gave him a death stare. But fortunately for her, he had stared death in the face, and it didn't frighten him.

"Did you make it?"

"Well, yes."

"Then you can repair it. And next time, it won't poke your boyfriend."

"What boyfriend?" She glared at him once more, and he thought an angry Heather Skye looked adorable. He swung his arms under her legs and swept her off her feet.

"What are you doing, Mr. Reilly?"

He smiled. "I'm holding onto you, because I've met no one like you, and I never will again."

"You're impossible!"

"No. It is impossible to let you go. But I'll compromise. How about if I set you on the bed?"

She glared at him again, but this time with a mischievous glint in her eye. "To put me in a compromising position? Do I get a choice in this?"

"Only if you give me a reasonable answer."

"Hmm," she said. "And I suppose a reasonable answer is 'Take me, Callum, and make me scream.'"

"Sounds perfectly reasonable to me."

"And how do you propose to do that?"

"First, I start by placing you on the bed, ever so gently." He laid her down and then stared at the perfection of her body. Her leather outfit accentuated every luscious curve, and her red mouth begged for kisses.

"Gentle, what a concept," she said.

"I see what I must do now," he replied.

"What is that?" He placed one knee on the bed and leaned forward to touch his lips to the swell of her breasts above the corset. He let his lips whisper-touch her neck, leaving a trail of kisses on her sweet flesh. She sighed and threw her arms around his neck, and pulled him down onto her body.

Taking the invitation, Callum claimed her lips and devoured her mouth with deep, sweeping strokes. Under him, she sighed louder and arched her back as he lowered his body onto hers. His pulse raced, and his thinking muddled from her scent and the delicious way her curves melted into him. God, how he wanted to feel her body squirm under him and listen to her moans of pleasure. It wasn't enough to get her off. He needed to possess every inch of her, inside and out. It occurred to him he could take a lifetime exploring her body and still not get enough of her.

He moved his hand between her leather-coated legs and stroked her, and felt the heat there. She whimpered and bucked her hips. It was glorious, and he wanted more—so much more.

But he also wanted her so hot that she'd beg him to come inside her.

Her breasts moved under her corset as her breathing quickened. With a smile, he teased out a breast and lowered his mouth to the succulent nipple. He lashed it with his tongue, and it peaked, hard and yet tender. She murmured incoherently. He sucked hard, and her back arched higher. Her responsiveness scrambled his brain. His breathing hitched, and his cock throbbed. He imagined sliding between her legs into her heat.

His hands engulfed her round ass as he reached for the laces that denied him her body. She shivered as he found the leather bow and tugged at it to open them.

"You are so fucking hot," he said.

She whimpered again as he slid the leather encasing her hips and legs down her thighs, as fasr as her high boots would allow. His hands trembled as her feminine musk hit his nose. He nuzzled the inside of her thigh. "Ooh, scratchy," she murmured.

"Problem?"

"Who do you think you're talking to?" she huffed. "God, no. More."

He was eager to oblige. "Yes, Miss Domme. Nice to know you can take it, as well as dish it out."

"I promise you'll find out more about the 'dishing out' part."

The idea of submitting to her type of sex didn't immediately appeal to Callum, but he liked her suggestion that there would be more between them.

"Good," he said. "I like promises."

He licked his lips as he gazed at her opening, which flushed with a rosy glow and filled with her cream. He lowered his head once more and licked her delicious juices, and he had to have more. As her breathing raced, his tongue lapped her opening, and then, drawing in her taste, dove inside her as she thrashed her head.

"Oh, fuck!" Heather screamed as she clenched her legs around his head. She drove her hips into his face, demanding more, and he delivered, delving deep while she thrashed on his face. Her channel pulsed around his tongue, and he couldn't wait until he plunged inside her.

Finally, she quieted, and he pulled away.

"Damn, Detective," she huffed. "You sure know how to get me wet."

He smiled. "Speaking of—"

But Heather sat up quickly in alarm and glanced toward the bedroom door. "Did you hear that?" she whispered.

He turned his head toward the door, toward the creak of a floorboard as if someone stepped on it.

He scrambled from the bed, and she swung her legs off quickly and tugged her leather slacks over her hips.

He waved her toward her bathroom, and she shook her head furiously "no." He didn't have time to argue, so he pushed her toward the wall by the door, then pulled his gun from his holster. He strained his ears to catch any sound.

"Both of you come out of there. I've got me and two guys with their guns pointing at your door."

Heather pushed past Callum in a rush and pulled open the door with her eyes blazing.

"Heather, no!" he whispered fiercely.

"Who the hell—oh you. The guys who ruined my back door." She spoke with loud indignation.

"Where's the cop?"

"I don't know what you're talking about. I'm alone here."

"Sure, and I have a bridge to sell you."

Through the crack between the open door and the jamb, Callum spotted the fat bastard and the two men with him pointing guns at Heather. Frustratingly, the smart play here was to watch Heather and rush to her defense if these guys didn't buy her act. It was a dangerous game, but Heather didn't flinch. He had to admire her bravery, but her actions were foolhardy.

"Get out of my apartment."

"From where I stand, missy, you are in no position to demand anything."

The man stepped forward and grabbed Heather's hair.

"How dare you!" She tried to squirm from his grasp, but her face twisted in pain as he continued to hold her hair.

"Shut up and be still. Cop, come out before I twist this hair off her little head."

"Try it, jerk," snarled Heather. She kicked into the gangster's groin. He howled, and his associates ran forward, but Callum rushed to the doorway and pointed his gun at them.

"Heather, get in here now," Callum ordered.

She tried to move forward, but the gangster grabbed her arm and twisted it behind her back.

"You bastard."

"What a foul mouth you have."

"Screw you." The fat man shoved her forward.

"Cop, drop your weapon, or I'll break her arm."

"Don't listen to him, Callum. I've had worse things happen."

Callum admired her feistiness, but these were not men to mess with. They wanted something, or rather someone, and it was him. He couldn't let Heather face danger on his account.

He held up his hands. "Okay. Just release her."

The man laughed. "Not a freakin' chance. You're both coming with us."

## 22

Usually, the lemon-oil scented woodwork of the apartment's halls and staircase lent a calming atmosphere to the building. But on this morning, with a gun pointed at Heather's back, her heart raced as the thugs escorted them down the stairs of the apartment. Even if she survived this day, she couldn't return here. Twice, intruders had breached her peace and security in this place, and she couldn't tolerate that.

Because her former roommate, Kristal, had to hide from a man with a vendetta against her, they had constructed elaborate security measures to keep Kristal safe. Now, with Kristal's problems resolved, married, and living with her husband, Heather thought those measures unnecessary. But with cold metal poking her spine, she realized she had been foolish. New York City was not a city in which to take safety for granted.

Her mind raced with different options. She could scream when she hit the street, but that wouldn't draw attention in this quiet neighborhood. She had kept her whip down her back under her corset, but if she moved too quickly, the jerks could turn gun-happy and catch Callum in the fallout.

The thugs hadn't tied her hands yet, but she could handle

that. Only someone with Master William's mastery of ropes could keep her bound. But that didn't answer the question of how they would escape their captors.

She glanced over her shoulder and caught Callum's eye. He shot her a cocky wink as if everything was OK.

"Hey, skank, eyes forward."

"Takes one to know one."

"Bi—"

The guy in charge swore.

"Stop talking, both of you. And move it, lady. I don't have all day."

"Hey, I'm missing a beauty appointment for this little sortie, so don't talk to me about inconvenience."

"Not much they can do for you, anyway," said the guy pointing a gun in her back.

"Shut up," the boss said.

"I didn't mean anything, Sal."

"Madre di Dio, you're stupid. Keep your mouth shut."

Heather had reached the bottom of the stairs. Her next step would place her boot on the shiny hexagonal tiles. She tried to peer over her shoulder again, but her guard dug his gun into her back more sharply.

"Hey, easy with that thing. We aren't even Facebooks friends, and even then I wouldn't let you poke me."

This time, warned by his superior, her nameless guard didn't speak. But Sal did.

"Shut up, whore."

"If I were, you couldn't afford me. I can tell by your cheap shirt. They say crime doesn't pay. I can see that now."

"Shut the fuck up," Sal said. Frustration seeped from his too-loud voice. Good. Rattling a guy was a good way to keep him off-balance.

"You might want to keep your voice down. My super lives in the apartment at the door on the left."

"When I'm done with you, your smart mouth won't look so pretty."

"Ooh, I'm shaking in my thigh-high boots."

"Madre, you are thick in the head. Move!"

Heather reluctantly set her boot on the foyer floor. She considered faking a fall because the thought of jabbing her stiletto heel in her guard's groin had enormous appeal. But there was Callum to consider, in more danger, with not one but two guns behind him.

"Move it," growled Sal.

Heather took a calming breath and stepped on the floor, and moved toward the front door.

"Not that way," Sal said. "Turn right and head toward the service hallway."

That would lead to the alley where the dumpster sat. It was a tight space, and if they pulled a vehicle in, it would be too small for anyone to move around.

She pursed her lips as she stepped into the hallway that ran from behind the stairwell to the outer wall. There were two of them, and three of the kidnappers, who were armed, but this place was a choke point. The people with the greatest level of skill had an advantage. These overweight and under-skilled thugs were not the people with the edge.

She glanced again at Callum, whose hands were clenched and his face unreadable. Callum did not let an opportunity go wasted.

She pushed her fingers down the back of her corset as if to scratch an itch.

"Jesus Christ on a stick," spat her captor. He pushed her head into the metal door and yanked on the security lever.

*Good*, thought Heather. The alarm would bring the police.

But her hopes shattered when the door opened and the only sound she heard was the door's creaky hinges.

*They must have disabled the alarm.*

"Push that fucking door wider, or I'll smash your head in again."

Reeling, Heather leaned against the heavy metal door.

"Run, Heather! Get help!"

She glanced over her shoulder and spotted Callum jabbing something into his first attacker's neck. Her eyes widened when she realized it—he was clutching the stay from her bustier.

"Go!" he screamed. Then Callum grabbed Sal's head and yanked on it to tumble him over the guy who held a gun on him. The man who kept Heather at gunpoint rushed to aid his compatriots.

"Go, woman!" Callum yelled.

She couldn't help, so with regret, she stumbled out the door and ran down the alley. She raced hard before turning left on the street, toward the direction of Central Park, with her head pounding. Since it was before dawn, the street was deserted. She didn't even see a dog walker. Her stiletto boots ground into her heels, which acted as a half blessing since the pain focused her attention.

*Find someone to help Callum.*

But she saw no one, and a screaming woman in the street would only draw stares.

*Where are the police when you need them?*

She neared a subway entrance but realized she had no money or her subway pass. A taxi passed by, but wouldn't halt for a wild woman with magenta-tipped hair.

She stopped because her breath ripped through her in ragged gasps, adding to her lightheadedness. Another taxi neared, and she stood and waved him down.

Gratefully, the taxi stopped, and Heather climbed in.

"Where to?" the driver asked.

She gave him William Ianucci's Park Avenue address.

"Where's your card?"

"My friend will pay you when we arrive."

"I don't know—"

"I promise."

"I wouldn't but for the address. But if you don't, I will have you arrested."

*That's okay, too*, she thought. The sooner she got to the police, the sooner she could help Callum. God only knows where those criminals were taking him. She hoped Master William could get some info from his "connections."

"I understand. Please hurry."

The cabbie grunted but started the taxi, and soon they pulled up to Master William's condo.

"So what now, lady?"

"I'll go in and stay inside that door where you can watch me. If I disappear, and I won't, you know where to send the police. I'll have the doorman call my friend down."

William Ianucci appeared in the lobby looking sleepy and harried.

"Miss Heather, what is going on?"

"Please pay my cabbie, Master William. I'll pay you back."

He scoffed. "Nonsense." He pulled a fifty from his wallet and gave it to the doorman. "Take care of that for me, Robert. I'm taking Miss Heather upstairs."

"Sure enough, Mr. Ianucci."

William put his arm around Heather and steered her to the elevator. When they entered, he said, "You are looking pale."

"Might be from the head-bashing. But I'm okay. It's Callum that is in trouble. Some Mafia thugs tried to kidnap us both. He fought them and told me to escape, so I did. I didn't want to leave him."

William nodded. "I'm sure you didn't, but Callum is a soldier. He'll know what to do to get through this. Who were these guys?'

"I don't know. Sal was one name."

"Salvatore is a popular Italian name. That is not much help."

Master William guided Heather into his apartment and Samantha came from the bedroom wrapped in a pink silk robe.

"Get some ice, sweetheart. Miss Heather got hit in the head."

"Heather, are you okay?"

"Yes."

"No. She's had a terrible experience. Ice, sweetheart?"

"Right away."

He led Heather to the L-shaped leather couch and urged her to sit.

"Honey, bring my phone."

"Sure," Samantha called from the kitchen area. The hollow crunch of ice from the refrigerator traveled across the room.

Soon, Samantha returned with the towel-wrapped ice and William's phone.

"Thanks, babe. Now, Heather, tell me what happened."

Heather placed the ice on her head and relayed the entire story from when the goons invaded her apartment. When she finished, William thumbed his phone.

"Uncle Gitchy? We have a problem. Does the guy we talked about earlier with Detective Reilly have a crew member by the name of Sal? Why? Because they kidnapped Detective Reilly about an hour ago. Okay, I'll wait for your call."

"Wait. You talked with Gitchy?" Heather said.

"Yes. But the less you know about it, the better."

"Master William, don't you dare try to protect me. I'm in the middle of this, and I need to know who I'm facing."

"You don't need to face a thing from this point forward.

When Uncle Gitchy calls back, he and I will take care of the situation with Callum."

"Why?"

"Because all of this has stirred up all the major families. The idea that one of them got involved with a terrorist organization has them all lit up. That the bad actors kidnapped a government investigator will send them into a fever pitch. Everyone still remembers the sweeps of the seventies when major and minor players got arrested in mass numbers. The families want to avoid involvement with the Feds. And that someone ventured onto forbidden ground, well, there could be war. Gitchy and I are trying to avoid that. It's bad for everyone's business."

Heather drew her lips tight. Samantha had said that William got his family out from under La Familia.

"Samantha said you aren't part of that world, anymore. Why would you put your neck out?"

"Because these guys messed with my friends. No one messes with my people, Miss Heather. I'm surprised you don't know that about me."

"I do. But what will Gitch—I mean, what will Dr. Russo do?"

"Get the info we need."

"Like where Callum is?"

"Where he could be, and who he might be with."

"Then you could call the police?"

"What, and have a SWAT team and snipers encircling the building? No. That would only get Callum killed."

Samantha moved to stand before her husband.

"And what exactly do you propose to do, William Ianucci? I told you that if you stepped one toe inside 'family business,' we were quits."

"Samantha, sweetheart—"

"Don't 'sweetheart' me, William."

"Samantha, if there is a war between the families, no one is safe. You don't want to know how bloody it will get. We'd have to move, and that would mean hauling up roots and leaving behind our business family and friends, good friends like Heather and Kristal. Do you want that?"

"I don't want my husband hurt, or killed."

William stood and kissed his wife.

"I have no intention of getting hurt or killed. Uncle Gitchy will bring assistance, and then we'll finish this business with those of us that would betray our country."

## 23

With another blow to the jaw, Callum's head reeled. He was extremely glad that Heather had escaped because these men were vicious. It disgusted him how they spoke to her at the apartment. He doubted she would have fared well in their hands.

He hoped that she had found help, because the blows to the head she suffered must have affected her. He'd worried on the van ride, to wherever this was, that she might have passed out on the street. Strenuous physical activity and head blows did not go well together.

At this point, Callum wasn't sure he'd make it through the day. They had tied his hands behind his back and his ankles, and made him kneel. With one of them watching him every second, he had no hope of breaking his bonds. And if he did, the space, an abandoned factory floor, was large and empty enough not to give him the cover needed.

*Heather, darling, I hope you are okay. I'm sorry that I put you through this. I'm so glad you escaped, and I wish I was more honest with you.*

He regretted putting Heather in the middle of his search for

Red Talon's money launderer. In his zeal to get at the truth, he put an innocent civilian at risk. And this time, the civilian didn't ask for the privilege of helping him.

*When will you learn, Reilly? How many people must get harmed because you charge bullheaded into a situation?*

The slow pace of his investigation had frustrated him. And he blundered when he insisted that Ianucci was part of the scheme despite having zero evidence for his assumptions.

He glanced through swollen eyes at the thug applying his "interrogation skills." With the last hit, Callum's eyesight blurred. It was not a good sign.

He spat out the blood trickling down his throat. "I tell you, Red Talon brings its A-game when roughing up people. Some have even lost their heads. I can sympathize with why you'd rather not screw this up. You'd prefer not to end up as an object lesson."

"Shut your pie hole."

"Talk, shut-up, talk, shut-up. I've argued with less annoying girlfriends."

"Wait until we bring your special girlfriend in. Perhaps you'll have something useful to say when we drag the whore before you."

"Sal. The boss wants to see you." A grating voice spoke from the shadows in the large room that Callum guessed was a shuttered factory. A dim light was switched on at the end of the room, displaying an office walled off from the main floor. Sal, the man who'd used him for a punching bag, walked to that light.

If Callum could swallow hard, he would. Did they recapture Heather? He could only hope that she located Captain Watrous to secure help for him. If not, at least she was safe. He believed that Master William wouldn't let anyone mess with Heather.

He had believed that William was a crime boss, but William

Ianucci only looked out for his family, business, and friends. Callum would apologize to the Dom if he survived this day.

Right now, from the sharp pain in his ribs, he had at least two cracked ribs, and from his nausea and dizziness, probably a mild head injury. How many blows to the head could he take? He didn't want to find out, but he resolved to last as long as possible until he blacked out.

One minute at a time.

That's what his informant had said while she and he were captives of Red Talon in Afghanistan. They wanted information from him, and he refused to give it. So she paid the price with her life.

Callum never resolved his guilt over that incident. Had he not made her an asset, had he not persuaded her to inform on her father, had he not met her that last time, she'd be alive.

The VA shrinks said it wasn't his fault. He didn't agree.

*Seriously, Callum, the girl had her reasons. Didn't you tell me her father planned a marriage for her to a man she despised?*

*Yes, but—*

*She knew the risks, probably better than you. She wanted to help you. We do things in a war that aren't pretty, but more people would die if we didn't.*

There were things that a soldier did in a war that weren't acceptable in normal society, but watching a teenage girl murdered by her own family shouldn't be one of them.

When the gangsters confronted them at Heather's place, he should have been more prepared. Aaron had told her that someone broke in. He should have checked out the apartment, surveilled the area, and searched for suspicious characters. Heather could have been seriously injured, or perhaps killed, for his lack of caution. His foolish lust for her made him mess up.

*Hell, it's not lust, Reilly, and you know it.*

He grimaced. He had never felt the emotions he experienced with Heather with any other woman. She was an irresistible force that drew him despite his instincts not to get close to a woman. Even with their differences, being with her felt more right than the few women he had dated.

*She's the one.*

The thought struck him like a sledgehammer, and it was probably because he sat on his knees with his hands behind his back, at the mercy of thugs who prayed for his death. He might not see tomorrow's sun and that didn't upset him as much at the thought of not seeing Heather again, and telling her he loved her.

*When did that happen?*

He had watched this leather-clad, self-possessed woman in action more than once. While he was attracted, he thought it was because he found her "bad girl" image alluring. Now, he figured out he had it wrong. It was her strength and grace that captured his attention.

"What the fuck," said a rougher voice.

In walked a man that Callum had not met.

"Hey, Jacko," the torturer said.

Callum sucked in a wheezy breath, even though it hurt to move his ribs. This was the man Gabriel Russo had fingered as laundering money for Red Talon—Giacomo Costa, otherwise known as Jacko the Bookie.

"Don't 'Jacko' me, asshole. Why does he look like that?"

"He won't talk, boss."

Jacko strode into the cavernous room and glared contemptuously at Callum. He stopped before Callum, towering over him. Maybe Jacko thought he'd intimidate by standing over him. Jacko was wrong.

Callum's ears rang, and he had trouble focusing.

Yeah, head injury for sure, the room spun, and his stomach

was nauseous. He laughed at the idea of spilling his guts on this jerk's shoes.

Things went hazy for a moment, and he swayed on his knees.

Someone slapped his cheek, not forceful enough to hurt, but he did squint his eyes together.

"Hey, cop. Wake up."

"Sure, sure," he mumbled.

"Something's wrong with him."

"He's faking."

"Let me see his eyes."

Someone roughly raised an eyelid and swore. Callum winced despite his training not to display pain or fear.

"His pupils are dilated. I saw it with fighters when I was making book. What the fuck did you do, Sal? We needed him to tell us who is squealing to the police. We must kill that rat."

*Interesting,* thought Callum. He would love to know who squealed to the police because, as lead on this investigation, he should have been told about an informant.

*Find that guy who took the informant's intel, and you'll have your man, or at least one of them,* thought Callum. But beaten so he couldn't stand, with hands tied behind his back, he didn't know how he would escape this situation.

"Naw, boss."

"Don't give me that BS," Jacko said. "There is no way that we'd have all this heat on us if there weren't a snitch."

"One cop—"

"One cop sent by the Feds, asshole."

Callum grimaced. And where did that piece of information come from? Few people in the department knew of Callum's connection with NCIS. Watrous, of course, but Callum would swear the man was a straight arrow and not on the take. But it was good to play on Jacko's fears to get him shook up and maybe spill what info he had.

"Hey, Jacko. I recognize you from your mugshots," Callum said.

"Shut up, cop," snarled Jacko.

Callum sighed. "Here we go again. Shut-up, talk, shut-up, talk. It's like a low-scoring ping pong game."

"Who sicced you on me?" Jacko said.

Callum laughed, though he ended up coughing, causing more pain to spread through his midsection. He needed to pry more information from this guy, so he used what little Gabriel Russo told him.

"Why do you think that? Because you spread rumors about William Ianucci to get back at him for ejecting you from the bookie trade in NYC, and your scheme didn't work?"

What Russo couldn't tell Callum was how that information infiltrated the Chi-town precinct or who did it. As the instigator of this plan, Jacko had to know who their agent was. And he could trust no one at the precinct until he figured out who that jerk was.

"You think he's using me to get back at you? Tell me. Did you *ever* graduate high school?"

"He fucking deserved it. I earned for that family."

"Did you ever think that more than one associate of the Nicero crime family had it out for you, Jacko? From what I heard, you crossed the streams with the Praegano operation and the Ianucci organization and then into the Puerto Rican gangs. Dogs, wasn't it? You bet too heavily on the dogs, so you had to skim from both of them."

"Who told you that?" snarled Jacko.

"Everyone knows that, Jacko. Hell, it's written on your jacket in the precinct house."

Jacko's eyes looked they would bug out from their sockets

and his cheeks flamed red. It was an embarrassing story. Nicero had all but disowned Jacko.

Or had he? Jacko wasn't smart enough to pull off a large operation and he must report to someone.

"I'll bet your boss isn't too happy with you right now."

"Shut the fuck up! Ianucci and Praegano were just two-bit operations."

"That's right. And when given a chance to betray your country and launder money for a terrorist organization, you jumped. Only, you're too stupid to pull this off on your own. Who is your boss? Who are you fronting for?"

That earned Callum another crack on his jaw, and his head snapped back as pain raced through it. He held his breath, hoping the idiot would spill his guts. But he wasn't that lucky.

"That's it. Sal. There's no getting any information from him. Make sure your crew snatches the whore when she gets home. No telling what this asshole told her. When we have both of them, we'll dump them at sea."

Callum hoped Heather would stay away from the apartment. He prayed she'd reached people that would help her. All he wanted was for her to be okay and away from the mess he brought on her.

He closed his eyes.

"I'm sorry, Heather."

Sal stepped behind Callum and grabbed his collar.

"Stand up," he growled.

Callum, with Sal yanking the collar upward, stood shakily on his feet. He drew another painful breath.

"Get going," Sal said roughly. He spun Callum to face a door opposite the front of the decrepit factory.

They walked to the door, and Sal opened it slowly, then he shut it like the door handle was on fire. Sal then shoved Callum against the wall and held his arm across his throat.

"Boss! We've got trouble!"

"What?" Jacko said. He walked toward them, huffing with the strain of moving his large body.

"I see cars out there."

"Police?"

"No. But there's a black limo out there."

## 24

"Okay, Heather," Master William said. "You have one job. Once we get inside, call the police and get them here."

Heather took a bit of slice of the pizza that William had brought "just in case," and glanced at the decrepit red-brick building that was once a factory in NYC's Long Island City section. Once a manufacturing hub, despite reclamation efforts, many of its once-productive buildings festered by the East River waterfront. This building, covered in graffiti, appeared all manner of unsafe. And they were the single vehicle parked behind an abandoned truck because the men Dr. Russo had promised had not yet arrived.

"I want to go with you."

William shook his head. "I need someone out here I can trust to bring in the reinforcements. The guys Uncle Gitchy will bring in will take off when they hear police sirens. And we need to get the guys that kidnapped Callum in police custody."

"I still think we should call them now."

"Heather, the police deal too heavy a hand. I told you that."

"Yes, between SWAT vehicles and snipers, Callum doesn't have a chance. You told me."

"Good. I'm glad you understand."

Heather pursed her lips. Master William's trust didn't outweigh her need to see Callum safe. But she'd sit tight because she knew the stakes. Master William had laid them out in stark detail. But if she had her druthers, she'd march in there and pull Callum out.

"When will they get here?"

"When Uncle Gitchy obtains permission for today's activities."

"What's taking so long?"

"Heather, getting the say-so for this type of operation isn't an easy thing. First, the families need to reach a consensus, and even if they do, the big boss could vote it down. Second, it's a good thing that Jacko isn't a made man. That would make this nearly impossible."

Heather disliked that a bunch of nameless men held Callum's life in their hands. From her viewpoint, if they had been watching their business, none of their associates would have slipped into dealing with enemies of the country. She'd love to know who screwed up.

"And the big boss is?"

"A name you don't need to know."

Heather drew a deep breath to calm her nerves. She didn't pretend to understand the world from which Master William came. The world he'd tried to get free from. She regretted her part in dragging him back in.

The crunch of vehicles rolling in on the broken pavement drew her attention. A black limo pulled behind them, and Gabriel Russo stepped out. William rolled down the window.

"Okay, I got twenty guys from different crews. Not a single boss took responsibility for Jacko, so that's not good. I don't know if all the guys here are working for us. So I mixed up the crews and got all sides of the building covered, and they know not to touch the cop. We go when I send the signal on my cell phone."

William nodded. "I understand."

"And you need to stay in the car. This is family business, and you wanted out, remember?"

"I'm responsible for Detective Reilly," William insisted.

Russo shook his white-haired head.

"The bosses don't see it that way. We'll get him out, in the name of goodwill, but you can't take part. Listen to me, Gil. They are keeping to their part of the deal you made. Keep to yours."

"Fine," William said. He huffed with dissatisfaction.

Just at that moment, the door opened, and a head poked out, then the door shut quickly.

"Looks like we've been found out," Gitchy said.

"*Matrona*," William swore. "This will make it harder. We need to go, now."

"Good," Heather said. She handed William the phone he'd given her to call the police.

"What are you doing?"

"Look, guys, how do you expect to get in there? They are locked in tight. A pretty girl opens doors."

"Heather, don't—"

"My mind's made up. But don't worry. Callum says my outfits are deadly." She winked at William and Dr. Russo, and sprang from the car, after snatching up the pizza box on the seat between them.

"Who says 'no' to pizza? It's a worldwide language. When the door opens, tell your guys to hit it."

She didn't wait for either man to reply. She held the pizza box high to cover her face and trotted to the door that had opened seconds before. She knocked hard on the metal and prayed it would open.

The door creaked as it swung from the doorjamb.

"Somebody here order some pizza?" Heather said in a Jersey Shore accent. "'Cause this a weird place to deliver one, and I hafta get back to the shop. Bobbie hates manning the register alone."

"Pizza, yeah. Somebody probably did. What's your name, sweetheart?"

"Joey, what the hell are you doing?" rumbled a voice in the background.

"Did you order a pizza, Sal?"

"Fuck no, asshole."

"Too bad," Heather said. "Because someone is paying."

Heather dropped the pizza and pulled out her whip, and hooked it around Joey's neck. The slob tried to turn and run, but she was too quick. She yanked back hard, and the man reached for the noose around his neck, sputtering, coughing, and struggling against the leather.

"Get her!" Sal yelled. But she kept her victim between herself and the three men coming at her.

"I'll kill him, I swear," Heather said.

"Who fucking cares?" Sal rumbled.

Heather spotted Callum on the floor. At the sound of her voice, he lifted his head, but he was solidly bound.

"Dude, we have to work on your rope skills."

"Get out of here, Heather."

"Nope. No one messes with my man. And these assholes will learn to respect Mistress Heather."

At that second, Dr. Russo walked in. He winked at Heather.

"You've got guts. Now, you, Jacko, get your lazy ass out here."

Jacko walked from the office.

"What do you want, Russo?"

"The bosses and I had a chat this morning. You're done for. I've got a deal for you and the choice is walking out of here alive, or not. I have a bunch of guys from different crews out there, and they'll shoot on sight anyone who runs out of here. Drop your gun, and you'll live. Act like a *stunad* and you don't."

"To hell with this," said the fourth guy in the room. He ran for the other side of the building, and soon shots rang out.

"Get it, Jacko. Toss your guns out of the way, and you, Sal, and Baby Dumpling here line up against the wall."

"Baby Dumpling?" Heather said.

"Seemed appropriate. Wannabe gangster." He turned his attention to the gangsters. "Drop 'em, or I'll call the guys in."

Jacko glared at Russo, but he dropped his gun, and then Sal did. They put their hands on the wall after shooting glares at Heather and Russo.

Russo bent and picked up a discarded gun. He pointed it at the captive.

"You can let Baby Dumpling go, Heather. He's not going anywhere, are you?"

The man shook his head, and Heather let the leather slacken, then let it slide like a snake from his neck. When released, he hurried to the wall and lined up with the other two men.

Heather ran to Callum and pulled the ropes loose. She stood then and went to the three men and tied their hands behind their back.

"Ouch," Sal said when she pulled the last rope tight.

"Don't struggle and you might keep the function of your hands. Besides, the police will be here any minute and put proper cuffs on you."

"Police? Russo, you said I'd get out of here alive," Jacko said.

Police sirens sounded in the distance.

But Russo didn't answer, and when Heather looked toward where Russo had stood, he was gone.

Heather smiled and cracked her whip on the concrete with a big grin. "He's not hanging around, but I am, so behave yourselves, boys, and I won't use my leather whip on you. I hope one of you tries something because I haven't had real fun with a whip in a long time."

But she didn't have time to carry out her threat because the back door swung open, and a stream of SWAT officers swarmed in.

"Over there, officers." Heather grinned as she held up her hands. "These guys, they kidnapped this detective, Callum Reilly, and tried to kidnap me."

"You did this on your own?"

She smiled again. "I'm very good with ropes. Now, excuse me. I'm going to see to Detective Reilly."

She knelt beside him and cradled his head in her lap. "You look horrible."

"And you look like an angel. An insane angel, but heavenly just the same." His voice came out scratchy and hoarse.

"How do you feel?" she asked.

"Like I look. Your hero?"

"Verifiable."

"Your man?"

"Undoubtedly."

"Forever?"

"Well—"

"Give a man a break," he said. "It's been a terrible day."

Heather pursed her lips.

"Okay. I don't usually do this—"

"Usually?"

"Well, never. Now shush and let me talk. Let's make a deal. We'll take things from here and reevaluate in a year."

Callum closed his eyes, and Heather thought he'd passed out. But then they fluttered open.

"I can live with that," Callum said. "Now, let's get me out of here."

## 25

### ONE YEAR LATER

Even though he was driving, Callum reached to touch the tips of Heather's hair.

"You didn't need to do that," he said. Callum referred to the recent dye job where Heather had washed out the magenta tips in favor of straight black. If the sun hit the strands just so, he could make out a hint of their former color. And she had removed all her piercings, too, except for one set of pierced earrings.

Heather gave a half-snort. "The way you describe your parents, I would say I did."

Callum glanced at the curve-hugging dress in a small floral pattern that she had donned. It was a shock to see her dress in such a conservative fashion. He missed her corset, leather pants, and boots that were as hot as hell.

"This is not the Heather Skye I know and love."

She gave him a saucy wink.

"Consider it cosplay, only instead of going to a BDSM club, or a medieval faire, we're going to Winnetka, Illinois, which seems like a kind of weird, conservative fairyland from what Mr. Internet said."

"Somewhat. We do have a music festival every year—real rocker music. You'd fit in fine wearing your usual clothes."

"Somehow that image is at odds with that tulip-filled small town vibe Winnetka's website displayed."

Heather was digging deep, and he had to turn her agile mind away from her line of inquiry. He adored her relentless spirit, but if he was to enact his plan, she had to be in the dark until the last minute.

"You have that right. But I'd love to see you show up at their door as Domme Heather Skye."

Heather gave him an incredulous glance.

"I don't plan on giving your father a heart attack, Callum. And I don't want to have to walk to the nearest bus stop if he threw me out."

"I'd never let that happen."

"And I won't let you blow a chance to patch things with your father."

He gripped the steering wheel tightly. Yes, he needed to see his father, though it wasn't a pleasant thought. He had to let his father know that he'd made Heather a permanent fixture in his life. If the old conservative coot didn't like it, oh, well. At least he would have tried.

"You look pensive, Callum."

He shrugged his shoulders. "I like who you are. Hiding it seems wrong."

"You just want to shock your father with me as natural Heather Skye."

Damn it. She was correct. Heather had an uncanny ability to see through a person's defenses. And the honesty she learned as a BDSM practitioner still surprised him on more than one occasion.

"What are you worried about? That he won't like me?"

"I don't care about that. I just want you to know that you

have zero need to be anything else but who you are on account of my parents."

"Don't worry. I don't plan to abandon my true self," Heather said.

He shook his head with a smile.

"I never thought you would."

"Besides, since meeting you, I'm not so much Domme Heather Skye."

Callum stared ahead. Navigating the relationship with Heather was tricky, but they had alternated roles and tossed in vanilla sex, too. It was a compromise that allowed both some of what they wanted. Heather switched roles like a champ. Once Callum got past the idea he might hurt her, he enjoyed the Dom role.

"You will always be Mistress Heather to me," he said.

Callum smiled as he stared at the road ahead. The sign for Winnetka flashed by.

"Almost there, babe."

"I see. Tell me what your hometown is like."

"Oh, like any other hometown."

Heather narrowed her eyes. "I know that tone. That and Mr. Internet tells me you're hiding something."

"I'm not," lied Callum.

"Then why won't you tell me your parents' address? Do they live in a shack on the wrong side of the tracks?"

She was far too good at internet searches. If Callum gave her his parent's address, she'd find out everything about them in ten minutes flat. Callum didn't flash his wealth to anyone and hated to think that she would look at him differently, especially since he didn't tell her upfront. Heather hated liars, and lying by omission was as bad to her as dissembling straight out.

"Would you care?"

"No, Callum Reilly, I would not. Which is why I wonder what secret you're hiding from me." She crossed her arms and glared at him. This conversation was rapidly becoming uncomfortable. He decided for the sake of his plans to deflect her attention.

"Okay, you got me. Both my parents live in the local mental hospital."

She slapped his arm.

"Liar!" she declared.

He chuckled. "You caught me."

She struck him on the arm again. "You're terrible."

"Then I deserve a punishment," he said with a wink.

She huffed and crossed her arms again. "Now, you're just teasing me."

He was. He still had trouble switching to the sub role. Too many things about it triggered unbearable memories, even when Heather treated him with exceeding care.

"Which is my favorite thing to do. Hey, we are coming up on the center of town. Doesn't look like it changed much. A couple of different shops."

"Looks picturesque. Where is your parents' house?"

"It's a small town. We'll be there soon."

She huffed and watched the houses as they drove past. There were lots of middle-class homes here — "Leave It to Beaver" types, with prices no higher than many New York apartments. But he could see by her expression that his tour of the tiny town, less than four square miles, didn't fool her.

Her eyes narrowed more as they turned onto Sheridan Road, where the houses had beaches on Lake Michigan, and were worth millions of dollars.

"Are you going to fess up to me now, Callum, or will I have to administer a thorough thrashing to your lying self?"

"I haven't lied. Just didn't tell the whole truth."

"Uh-huh," she said. Heather's expression conveyed her unhappiness. "I thought we put dishonesty behind us, Callum." She used her Domme voice, which could strike fear into the hearts of most men. But Callum knew what a pussycat his Heather was deep inside.

"Does my background matter than much?" he said.

"No. It does not. The lack of honesty does."

"Babe—"

"Don't 'babe' me. We've had this discussion. Now, I don't know what I'll do."

He was well aware of the problems that haunted her trust issues. She had told him how the first man she had loved lied to her about being married. When she became pregnant, he dropped her, and her very conservative parents made plans to send her away to a home for pregnant teens. Alone, frightened, and with no one to turn to, the stress caused her to lose the baby. It was a trauma from which she barely recovered, and which taught her running away was a good survival tactic.

"Well, just meet my parents first. And then you can decide what you want to do with me. Here we are."

Callum turned up a long driveway past manicured hedges and a lawn half the size of a football field.

"Not even an apology?" she sniffed.

"I won't apologize for where I came from and who I am." And he thought, *who you are.*

Heather sighed but framed her face with her pretty smile as the drive turned circular and they pulled to the front door. His mother must have been waiting by the door, because it opened immediately and there she stood.

"Callum! I'm so glad you're home."

Heather hung back as he walked to his mother and gave her

a hug. She seemed thinner and frailer than when he saw her last, but it had been ten years.

*Shame on me.*

"Lucretia has lunch ready," she said with a smile.

"She's still with you?" He couldn't believe Lucretia, a fixture in the house since his early teens, still cooked for his parents.

"One of the family, Callum. Though she plans to retire to Florida next year."

"And this is Heather," Callum said. He reached his hand out for Heather to take it, but his mother stepped forward and threw her arms around her.

"Welcome, welcome. I'm so glad to meet you at last."

"I can see where Callum gets his good looks," Heather said. Callum resisted the urge to shake his head. Once Heather was on a mission, she was unstoppable.

"Aren't you sweet? But Callum has more of his father in him. You'll see."

Callum cleared his throat.

"And where is Dad?"

"He's in the greenhouse with his orchids. He'll be in soon. Come, Heather, let me show you the house."

His mother led Heather away chatting happily to her, leaving him in the massive foyer alone. He might as well get this over with.

Callum walked to the back of the house where the greenhouse was attached to the main house. He found his father with a brush hand-pollinating several of the difficult-to-grow plants.

"Hello, Father."

His father didn't bother to turn toward him.

"So you finally came home," he said flatly.

"For a short time. Your orchids look good."

"It's an exacting hobby. Fortunately, I have time for it." Justus

Reilly laid the brush on his workbench and turned toward his son.

"And I hear you left the military."

"I did."

"In favor of working for the New York Police Department." His tone told Callum his father would be happier if Callum crawled under a rock and remained there.

"I like what I do. And I'm helping people."

"But again, you put your life at risk!" His anger took Callum aback.

"I assure you, I'm safer in NYC than in the military."

"You needn't be in either. Callum, you have enough money so you don't have to work."

This was always the problem. Callum wanted to contribute to the greater good, not suck of it like it was a milkshake.

"Come, meet Heather. I'm sure you'll like her." *She worked hard enough to turn into your kind of likeable.*

For a woman so devoted to honesty, she wasn't playing it straight today.

His father sighed as if he expected disappointment there, too.

"So there's no chance you'll come home for good. Your mother would like that."

*Not unless they have a nice BDSM club here.*

Callum ignored the jab. "Lead the way, Dad."

"Forgot your way around the house already."

Justus Reilly was in rare form today.

Hundreds of smart-ass remarks flittered through Callum's head, but no. He'd act the grownup. It was time he did.

"Dad, I'm sorry if I distressed you or Mom."

"Tell that to her."

*She's not the one that needs the apology.*

Lucretia had set up lunch in chafing dishes in the dining

room on the antique sideboard that stood under the room's bank of windows. The familiar aromas of his youth brought back difficult memories of life in his parent's house.

*If you don't like it, you can leave.* He had heard that so many times that he finally took his father up on his offer.

"Ah, there you are, Justus. This is Callum's girl, Heather Skye."

His father looked over Heather with a critical eye, as if to find something to fault, but then relaxed as if finding none.

"Welcome to our home, Heather."

"It's nice to meet you. Callum's told me so much about you."

His father's eyes scrunched up. "I don't see how he could. We haven't seen him for over a decade."

His mother intervened swiftly. "Now, Justus, let's have lunch. It's getting cold."

Just as he usually did, Justus Reilly deferred to his wife and took her hand. It was said on the North Shore that the only one who handle Justus Reilly was Amelia Reilly. Heather watched the exchange with interest.

Callum came behind Heather at the sideboard as she put food on her plate.

"Are they expecting more people? There is a ton of food here."

"No, just us."

"Your parents seem nice."

"And you are pulling off your act to perfection, Miss Honesty."

She scoffed, walked to the table, and settled in.

"Everything looks wonderful," Heather cooed.

She and his parents chatted for several minutes in a total un-Heather fashion.

"And what do you do for a living, dear?" his mother said.

"I run a shop," Heather said.

"Oh, what kind of store? A clothing store?"

Callum waited for what Heather would say.

"You might say that. I do have clothing items in it."

Callum had enough of this act. He loved Heather, the real Heather. He pulled out his phone. "Would you like to see some pictures of New York?"

"That would be lovely," his mother said.

Callum stood and walked the corner of the table, where his father sat at the head, and his mother sat catty-corner to his father.

"This is Heather at the club we frequent." Here Heather wore her signature leathers. Her corset was the magenta one that matched the tips of her hair.

"Callum," Heather growled.

His father stared at the picture. "Is this a Halloween party?"

"No, just our typical Thursday night."

"Typical?" his father said in disbelief.

"Oh, and this is a picture of her store. It caters to the BDSM crowd in New York. She makes the leatherwork they sell. And it's very exclusive. You need an invitation to enter."

His father's face blanched. "She owns this?"

"Well, she and her partner, with Master William as a silent partner." He glanced at Heather, who glared him through the fingers she splayed on her face.

"Let me see, son," his mother said. She took the phone and glanced at the pictures. Her response would have knocked Callum off his seat if he were sitting.

"That's a lovely outfit, Heather. Why didn't you wear it today?"

Heather dropped the hands from her face and stared at Amelia Reilly in disbelief.

"You know what that outfit is?" she asked.

"Of course, dear. I wish I had one half as nice. You have real talent there."

"Amelia," Justus protested.

"Oh, for heaven's sake, Justus, what did I tell you about acting like a prude?" She turned to Heather. "He's not, but somehow thinks he needs to keep up appearances."

"Wait. You and Dad are into kink?" Callum said.

His mother smiled and opened her mouth.

Callum held up his hand. "Wait, Mom. TMI. I don't need to know the details."

"I think that's best," his father said.

Heather laughed. "And here I was worried that I was too kinky for your family."

Both his parents began laughing too. Callum watched the scene in amazement, but there was something he needed to say.

"Well, now that your secrets are out, I guess I need to spill mine."

"You have more secrets?" Heather said with suspicion.

Callum walked to Heather's chair while fingering the box in his pocket and got down on one knee.

"It's no secret that I love you, Heather Skye. And I haven't been truthful with you. What I have been keeping from you is that I went shopping, with Kristal, so I wouldn't screw this up—"

"Callum, she just had a baby."

"She was glad to get out of the house. Now don't deflect." He retrieved the box from his pocket and opened it.

"Will you marry me, Miss Heather Skye?"

Heather swallowed hard as she stared at the three-karat ring. "Marriage?" she said. "I don't know. You can be very difficult, Callum."

"I'm sure you'll figure out a way to straighten me out. Say yes, Heather. Because you'll always be the mistress of my heart."

A tear slipped from the corner of her eye.

"Callum Reilly. There is no one else I would marry, so, yes."

"Wonderful," his mother said. "Just tell me one thing. Who's the bottom and who's the top?"

"Amelia!" her husband protested. "TMI!"

"It doesn't matter," Callum said. "As long as I'm with Heather, we'll work it out."

# MORE BOOKS BY JESSIE COOKE

Just like Grey Novels

Just like Grey Boxsets

Just like Grey Singles

---

Hot Mess - A One-of-a-Kind Romantic Comedy Action Adventure unlike anything you've ever read!

---

All My Books including MC Romance and Bad Boys at JessieCooke.com

Copyright © Jessie Cooke

**All rights reserved.**

No part of this book may be reproduced in any form or by any electronic or mechanical means, including information storage and retrieval systems, without written permission from the author, except for the use of brief quotations in a book review.

## License.

This book is available exclusively on Amazon.com. If you found this book for free or from a site other than Amazon.com country specific website it means the author was not compensated and you have likely obtained the book through an unapproved distribution channel.

## Acknowledgements

This book is a work of fiction. The names, characters, places and events are products of the writer's imagination or have been used fictitiously and are not to be construed as real. Any resemblance to people, living or dead, actual events, locales or organizations is entirely coincidental.

Printed in Great Britain
by Amazon